IDYLLIC INTERLUDE

BY
HELEN SHELTON

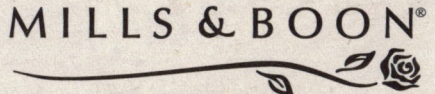

MILLS & BOON®

First published in Great Britain 2000
Harlequin Mills & Boon Limited,
Eton House, 18-24 Paradise Road, Richmond, Surrey TW9 1SR

© Poppytech Services Pty., Ltd 2000

ISBN 0 263 82225 7

Set in Times Roman 10½ on 11½ pt.
03-0003-54779

Printed and bound in Spain
by Litografia Rosés, S.A., Barcelona

'So now you're all alone.'

'I'm an adult,' Libby told Nathan quietly, looking up at him. 'I'm fully grown,' she added huskily. 'Hardly abandoned.'

'And, of course, you have Alistair.' He didn't give her a chance to question that because he'd stepped back, his expression utterly inscrutable. 'But Alistair's away, isn't he?' Nathan said evenly. 'So there's nobody to protect you.'

'I don't need protection,' Libby countered stiffly.

'I wonder,' he murmured.

A New Zealand doctor with restless feet, **Helen Shelton** has lived and worked in Britain and travelled widely. Married to an Australian she met while on safari in Africa, she recently moved to Sydney where they plan to settle for a little while at least. She has always been an enthusiastic reader and writer and inspiration for the background for her medical romances comes directly from her own experiences working in hospitals in several countries around the world.

Recent titles by the same author:

CHAPTER ONE

DANGLING a heart-shaped keyring and its two keys in the air behind his back, Alistair backed away from his brother. 'The family's buzzing with speculation,' he revealed teasingly. 'What none of us understand is why you're suddenly so keen on my little Cornwall hideaway. We decided you must be stricken with a mad passion for someone else's wife only the husband's the insanely jealous type and you're worried about getting caught.'

Nathan lifted his eyes briefly to the ceiling. 'Be reassured that I have never,' he said dryly, 'been stricken with mad passion.' He didn't bother attempting to conceal his amusement at the idiocy of such speculation. He liked women, *enjoyed* women, but his passions had never been anything other than controlled. 'You should be working for a tabloid, not a nature magazine,' he told the younger man with an easy grin. 'You've obviously got the talent. Come on, Ali. Keys, please. Theatre's waiting for me and you should be halfway to Heathrow by now.'

But his brother merely waggled the keyring so it jingled behind him. 'Just a hint,' he insisted. 'Satisfy my curiosity and they're yours.'

'You're curious because I'm taking a few weeks off?'

'Considering, Nate, that you never take holidays,' Alistair reminded him, 'yes, of course. We all are.'

Nathan sighed. 'Florida was a holiday.'

Alistair's eyebrows disappeared into his sandy fringe. 'Yes, when you graduated!' he yelped. 'I was about thirteen. I'm twenty-six now!'

'Then you understand why I need a break.' Refraining

5

from any comment about the fact that Alistair's current behaviour with the keys he needed was more in keeping with that of the cheeky teenager the younger man had once been, he said lazily, 'So?'

With a good-humoured sigh Alistair let the keys drop into Nathan's outstretched palm. 'These open the shed and the back door,' he told him. 'The one for the front door's under the flowerpot on the top step.' He laughed at Nathan's speculative look. 'It's Cornwall, Nate, not crime-infested London. Also, I've a good neighbour.' He tilted his head. 'Miles to the nearest hospital, though. Sure you won't get withdrawal symptoms?'

Resisting the urge to roll his eyes again, Nathan checked his watch, slid the keys into the inside pocket of his jacket, then opened his office door. 'Have a great trip.'

'Yeah, yeah.' With a grin that suggested he understood he was being dismissed, Alistair ambled towards the door, then just as Nathan was congratulating himself on getting rid of him at last the younger man stopped.

'I promised to ring Mum after I saw you,' he said. 'You know what she's like. For your sake, Nate, you'd be better off admitting you are taking a woman down there. Even Mum being mad with curiosity's better than the alternative. If they think you're going to be lonely, she and Dad are likely to drive straight down to Cornwall tomorrow morning and surprise you.'

'There's no woman,' Nathan said wearily. 'I'm going to be alone but not lonely.' But Alistair was probably right, he reflected. Fond as he was of his mother and her husband, and enjoyable as he found their company, he didn't need his mother's inquisitiveness, or her cleaning up around him and trying to cook his meals for him when he needed to work. He knew he'd been neglecting his family lately but when he returned from Cornwall with his research paper written up and ready to submit for publication, he'd make a determined effort to spend more time with them all.

'I need somewhere quiet to work,' he revealed easily. 'I won't have time for company. I'll call her tonight and explain.'

'Couldn't you do whatever you're going to do here?'

He'd been trying to for six months, but his clinical work had proven too great a distraction. 'I need peace,' he told him. 'In a month in Cornwall I hope to do what would take me six here.'

He didn't add that in an attempt to reduce the number of operations and conserve surgical funds the hospital was forcing him to take some of his accumulated leave. Although he despised the awareness that economic considerations were now stopping him from treating his patients, his opinions were best kept private. If his views became public knowledge doubtless he'd find even more restrictions on his expenditure. And while Alistair was currently working for an American wildlife magazine, he still retained connections within the British press.

'Well, my money's still on the wife and the jealous husband,' Alistair declared heartily, prompting a reluctant grin from Nathan. 'And don't think I won't find out because I've spies everywhere down there.' He checked his wristwatch. 'Right, I'm off.' He eased himself away from the doorframe and strolled through Nathan's secretary's office, winking at Mrs Langley before opening the door into the corridor. 'Have fun, whatever you're doing, Nate, and give my love to Libby. She knows the area much better than I do so she'll help you out if there's anything you need.'

'Libby?' Nathan queried quickly.

'The neighbour,' Alistair drawled. 'Oh, and, Nate?'

He'd hesitated in the outer doorway and Nathan looked up from a set of notes Mrs Langley had handed him. 'Hmm?'

'Hands off.'

Nathan grinned. Until recently Alistair seemed to have enjoyed playing the field, but Nathan had noted that his brother's life had grown more monastic. Alistair having found someone special would explain that. 'I'm being asked to keep my hands off…the neighbour?' he probed.

'Stick to your city women,' Alistair said cheerfully. 'Libby's too sensitive for the likes of you. Even if she wasn't the love of my life I wouldn't let you near her.'

'Ali, are you serious or—?' But the sudden blare of the bleeper from the pocket of his white coat distracted Nathan's attention. The illuminated number on the side showed that it was Theatres calling, and by the time he'd finished checking Alistair had lifted a hand in farewell and gone off down the corridor.

When he'd completed scrubbing and gowning and had moved to the operating table, he saw that his registrar and SHO together had opened their patient's abdomen, reflected most of the contents to clear the field for him and had exposed the renal arteries above the large aortic aneurysm. Nathan glanced at the arteriograms posted on the X-ray board, noting the ballooning of the aorta and clogged iliac vessels which were classic signs of advanced arterial disease.

'I don't understand why he presented so late,' he remarked, clamping and tying off a small artery which flowed from the bulging aorta and had to be sacrificed. 'From the state of those legs he must have had symptoms for years.'

'True, but he doesn't believe in conventional medicine. He wasn't even enrolled with a GP.' Richard, his registrar, rolled his eyes. 'Instead, he's been having his feet rubbed,' he explained, his tone mirroring Nathan's astonishment. 'Some crackpot therapist in a street market's been treating him with foot massage. Finally, when he can barely walk ten yards, his wife insists he see a doctor, who picks up the aneurysm.'

Nathan lifted his brows wryly. 'Another few weeks of foot massage might have been the end of him. We're operating just in time.' With Richard's help he cleared the lower part of the aorta where it bifurcated into the common iliac arteries, looping slings around the vessels. 'I don't suppose the crackpot bothered to tell him to stop smoking?'

Richard shook his head. 'Suggested a macrobiotic diet, though.'

They both laughed. 'That would have ensured his last days were miserable,' Nathan said lightly. Inwardly, though, the thought that the system had failed this man angered him. His experience told him that this aneurysm would have ruptured very soon if the patient hadn't finally been persuaded to come forward. 'We should all be grateful his wife has some sense,' he observed.

He couldn't get away from the hospital the next afternoon until twelve, and the lunchtime traffic was heavy heading back to his flat. By the time he'd showered and packed and set out again for the long drive down to Alistair's cottage it was mid-afternoon.

It was his own fault, he told himself ruefully, flicking his lights to allow a couple of queued cars out of a side street ahead of him. Having taken no holidays from St Stephen's in over four years, he wasn't used to not caring for his own patients. He could have left the hospital at eight that morning as he'd planned if he'd been willing to hand over care of his new admission to one of his colleagues.

Instead, after being up much of the night operating on a man who'd been brought in as an emergency with a ruptured abdominal aortic aneurysm, a vessel of similar size to the one he'd operated on the day before, he'd lingered. He'd found himself delaying his departure from the hospital until he'd been happy that his patient had been stable in the intensive care unit.

Although he knew his colleagues were more than able to look after his patients, he'd still found it—still *was* finding it—difficult to delegate responsibility. He'd left instructions with Richard to telephone him if there were any problems. Regardless of the surgical manager's instructions, he was prepared to drive or even fly up from Cornwall if he was needed.

He glanced at the phone he'd slung onto the passenger's seat, not knowing whether to be amused or appalled by his apparent inability to switch it off. But so far the device had stayed quiet and inwardly he was happy it would stay that way; his patient was a reasonably fit man and technically the surgery had gone well.

Finally on the M3 and heading south, the traffic cleared. His car handled well and he found himself enjoying the drive, and once he'd negotiated the string of roadworks which had closed off two lanes he had the road virtually to himself.

Privately, he reflected, although still irritated that the hospital's chief executive had forced the decision upon him, a few weeks away might do him good. As well as being on the transplant team, he was one of only two vascular surgeons at the busy teaching hospital and his on-call commitment was physically as well as mentally demanding.

Although, until the latest round of departmental budget cuts had started to bite, he'd always found his high workload stimulating rather than draining, now he was aware that he had been feeling more than mildly jaded.

While four weeks away from work seemed to him to be an excessive amount of time for a holiday—and probably two weeks more than he needed to prepare his data for publication, considering he'd be working on it full time—he reminded himself that he could always go back to St

Stephen's a week early. Even if the budget controllers wouldn't let him operate, he could catch up with some of his clinic cases.

Then he shook his head wryly. 'You're a sad case, Nathan Thomas,' he murmured. The first day of your first decent break in years and you're already anticipating rushing back to work.

A few hours later he turned off the main road and eased the car into the car park of a small pub. His body had stiffened during the drive and when he climbed out of the car he stretched appreciatively and drew in deep breaths of country air. He'd spent too much time in London, he decided, tasting the air's sweet freshness and wondering if his lungs were permanently soot-stained yet from living in the capital.

He had to stoop to enter the small pub. He knew the area had once been renowned for smuggling and, looking around, he found it easy to imagine contraband being exchanged, centuries before, in the dark and intimate interior. Mindful of the drive ahead, he ordered only a half of lager to go with his Cornish pasty. He returned the young barmaid's smile but gently ignored the flirtatious invitation in her eyes.

Despite Alistair apparently feeling some need to warn him off seducing his neighbour, his brother's concern had been unwarranted, he reflected, still amused by the memory of Alistair's pointed 'hands-off'. He was curious to meet his brother's Libby, of course, as curious as he'd be about meeting any of his siblings' potential wives or husbands. But regardless of how…irresistible Alistair found the woman, even if she hadn't already been involved with his brother, his own intentions would always have been merely friendly.

He wasn't celibate, but his sex life was satisfactorily orderly and arranged. Getting his work finished in the coming weeks was too important to him for him to be interested in pursuing any temporary romantic entanglement.

Despite following Alistair's instructions, he lost his way in the maze of tiny lanes leading to the cottage, and it was late twilight when he finally arrived. He parked the Saab outside and retrieved the key, finding it exactly where Alistair had told him he would—under a clay pot packed with fragrant pink and white flowers.

He grimaced, imagining what would happen to his Kensington flat if he left its key anywhere so obvious. The place would be looted within hours, he decided as he opened the stout wooden door.

He deposited his bags in what he assumed was Alistair's bedroom, the first room on the left as he stepped into the hall, then looked around assessingly, grinning at the cottage's startling decor. Working as a wildlife photographer, it meant Alistair travelled widely, and the rooms were decorated with Aztec-style wall-hangings and blankets and colourful African prints and photographs, and the comfortable furnishings and two huge Japanese-style futons were draped with warm, bright fabrics.

Alistair had managed to squeeze a shower cubicle into the cramped yet functional bathroom, and although the kitchen and sun room living area was small Nathan knew the space would be more than adequate for his needs.

The cottage had been neglected for years before Alistair had bought it and Nathan was impressed by his brother's efforts, as well as surprised by how much he liked the unorthodox style of decoration.

In fact, it seemed a vast improvement on his own expensive and professionally decorated London flat, he registered dryly, acknowledging that even if the flat *was* looted it would pose little more than an inconvenience to him. He carried insurance and, aside from some family photographs which his mother probably held copies of anyway, he couldn't think of any possessions he'd miss.

The realisation provoked a vague sense of discontent as he wondered briefly if his dissatisfaction at his work lately was beginning to spread to include the rest of his life.

Suddenly restless, he snapped open a lager from a supply he discovered in the kitchen, took a long draught and strolled outside through the back door and towards a grassy cliff at the back of the property. He stopped at the edge, taking a few deep breaths of the fresh sea air, enjoying the way the tang of salt at the back of his throat contrasted with the cool bitterness of the beer.

To call the view from the cliff breathtaking would have been a cliché but it seemed the only appropriate description, he acknowledged. Sunset had turned the sky burnt orange and gold, and in the fading light the sea was one huge, dark, glistening expanse stretching endlessly into the distance, its pale, frothing edge lapping a small beach in the cove below.

There was an overgrown hedge at the far left of the property and beside it he could see steps and a rocky path meandering down from the cliff towards the sea. Tempted to explore, he almost made for it before realising instead that it would be far more sensible to ignore the impulse and spend the rest of the evening setting up his computer and sorting his papers so he'd be ready for an early start to his work in the morning.

He'd been up much of the night before and the drive had been long. There'd be plenty of time for exploring and visiting the beach in the weeks ahead.

But as he started to turn back to the cottage he caught a movement out of his peripheral vision, and when he turned to examine it he realised he could make out a moving shape far out in the dark water.

Surely no one would be foolish enough to swim alone

at this time of the day? Although the sea looked calm, he knew that treacherous tides were common off this coast. The person might be in trouble, he realised, making a move towards the path.

As he reached the top of it the swimmer began heading purposefully toward the shore and he realised his help wasn't needed. She—and it was very definitely a *she* he could tell as the water became shallower and he could see the pale curves of her breasts beneath her moving arms— was obviously in no danger because her long, effortless strokes caused her to glide swiftly to the beach.

Within seconds she was standing in thigh-deep water. Nathan's eyes narrowed as she bent forward to unfasten her dark hair and he saw that her slender body was bare of any swimsuit. While he watched, she flung her head back and her hair cascaded down her back, clinging damply to her skin.

Obviously unused to observers, she moved through the waves utterly unselfconsciously and retrieved what looked like a towel from the beach. She was far enough away for him not to see details but he could tell that her body was exquisitely shaped. He watched her rub it briskly dry before she squeezed water from her hair and twined the towel around it like some elaborate headdress, leaving her bare again.

In the rapidly dulling light he knew he must be invisible from the beach. One part of him was appalled by the way he was invading the unknown woman's privacy, by watching her the way he was, but the other part, the part that seemed to be in control of his legs and good sense, didn't let him move away.

A mermaid, he thought faintly, before wincing at the tackiness of the imagery. But, tacky or not, at that moment he could understand how sailors might have been enticed to their deaths by such exotic creatures.

Too soon she disappeared from view beneath the overhanging cliff and then his legs and his conscience began working again and he strode deliberately and quickly back to the cottage.

Irritated by his illicit arousal, he took a brisk, cold shower, deliberately punishing his flesh by standing motionless under the chilling water until his desire faded. Knowing his chances of accomplishing any useful work that night were now almost nil, he towelled himself roughly dry and went to bed, surprising himself as almost immediately he felt his body sliding into sleep.

CHAPTER TWO

LIBBY woke to the sensation of something wet and cool in her ear. By the time she opened one sleepy green eye both her black cats were peering innocently at her from the rug beside her bed. She groaned. 'You rascals,' she said thickly, a weary look at the clock beside the bed telling her it was barely five-thirty. 'You absolute rascals. You know I won't be able to go back to sleep now.'

Resigned, but not yet fully alert, she slowly swung her legs to the floor, drew herself up then opened the heavy drapes across her window and flooded the room with soft morning sunshine. For late May the weather had been uncharacteristically warm, and with a lazy sound she raised her arms toward the ceiling, allowing herself a luxurious stretch in the glistening light.

But William promptly gave her leg a firm nudge. Laughing, Libby scooped up the silky creature, some of her normal energy returning to her limbs as she padded on bare feet into the kitchen to prepare breakfast for her pets.

Once they were feeding greedily, she dished herself a bowl of cereal and yoghurt and wandered out onto the porch of her small cottage, enjoying the blissful warmth of the morning sun's gentle rays on her body.

She never tired of the view from the cottage. The glorious expanse of sea and dark cliffs changed hourly with the light and season. No matter how often over the years she'd tried to capture the scene with her water-colours, every new painting she produced from here was different. And all were inspiring and comforting. Through long terms at boarding school and later during her nursing training she'd decorated the walls of her small rooms with those paintings. Little pieces of Cornwall to warm the grey London days.

This morning the sea sparkled glittering silver and Libby sighed her contentment, pleased now that the cats had awakened her early. Crying gulls dived for food where the water foamed against the cliffs but otherwise there was solitude and peace.

As she finished her breakfast her gaze drifted towards the cottage next door and she stood up, her forehead creasing. Alistair had said he'd be away at least a month but his bedroom window was open. He'd asked her to keep an eye on the cottage for him and while crime was rare in this part of Cornwall it wasn't unknown, particularly in the spring and summer months when tourists swelled the sparse local population.

She hurried inside. Her painting smock lay crumpled on the floor beside her bed and she slid it over her head, covering her nakedness. The cats had finished their breakfast and were sprawled in the sun in her room, washing each other. 'Alistair's probably offered the cottage to a friend,' she told them hopefully, but inwardly she was worried. He'd never done such a thing before without letting her know in advance.

Her neighbour's spare key in hand, she headed for the door. The cats followed her, their ears pricked up curiously, little black faces interested. 'Any burglar would have done the place over while it was dark and be miles away by now,' she told them confidently. Even so, she found herself grabbing a broom from behind the door before she crept stealthily through the gap in the hedge and towards Alistair's cottage, Duncan and William at her heels.

A soft weight on his chest and the brush of warm fur across his face jerked Nathan sharply awake.

'William!' he heard a woman whisper fiercely. 'Silly cat, come away!'

Bleary-eyed and dazed by the light streaming in through the window he'd left open the night before, Nathan found himself peering straight into the unblinking yellow eyes of a big black cat who stood solidly balancing on his chest.

He surged up onto his elbows and the creature immediately leapt away towards a girl who, he saw, was hovering uncertainly beside the door to his bedroom. His mermaid, he registered thickly, had not been a dream.

'I'm sorry.' The enticing, husky lilt of her low voice made his senses tauten alarmingly. 'He raced ahead when I opened the door.' The cat was sitting at her feet. Another, equally big and equally black, stood protectively beside it as if shielding its mistress, fixing him with a disturbingly flat golden glare which suggested it could read his thoughts.

And his thoughts were not the kind he'd want read, he acknowledged, bringing his knees up fast. The night before he'd sensed her grace and delicacy but close up he saw that she was beautiful. Cascading dark hair, her skin creamy pale aside from a light dusting of freckles over her little upturned nose, her almond-shaped green eyes obviously startled, she was enchantingly exquisite.

But his scrutiny obviously made her nervous because she'd backed away a little. 'I should go.'

'Where?' he demanded huskily, sitting up properly. 'Stop. What are you doing here? Who are you?'

'Libby Deane,' she told him, her first name enough to make him tense as he remembered Alistair's warning. 'From next door. I saw the window open,' she was saying. 'I just wanted to check....' She bit her lip, small white teeth puckering the soft flesh enough to drain its colour. 'I wanted to make sure everything was all right with the cottage.'

'Everything's fine.' Conscious of the increasing heaviness of his thighs, Nathan folded his arms abruptly around the sheet to make doubly sure he remained decently covered. 'I'm not an intruder.'

'Yes, I know. I saw Alistair's keyring on the table.' Her green eyes darted away from him then back again, as if he was still making her nervous but she didn't want to appear impolite. 'At first I thought you might be a burglar but then when I saw his keys…well, I knew you must be a friend.'

'Is the broom to fight off the burglar?'

'I suppose….' Her eyes flew back to his face, her expression embarrassed now. Defensively she held the broom behind her back as if by removing it from his view he'd forget it, and he promptly did, distracted by the unexpected glimpse of small, bare breasts lifting through the pale sheerness of her shift.

The sudden quickening of her breath suggested she'd sensed his interest and he jerked his gaze away, disgusted with himself for reacting to her so obviously.

But it was Libby who was apologising. *Alistair's* Libby, Nathan reminded himself savagely. 'I'm sorry,' she said again, 'but the cats rushed in and I had to fetch them first. I didn't mean to wake you. I'll leave now.'

'No! Libby, don't go.' He made an involuntary move towards her but remembered in time that he was naked beneath the bed coverings and…in a state that would no doubt appal her. He subsided back under the covers, making a small, impatient gesture with his hands. 'Wait. Please. In the kitchen. Let me dress and I'll come and join you. I won't be long.'

She still looked as if she'd have preferred to leave, and he knew that might be best, yet he still heard himself arguing. 'Make us a hot drink.' When she hesitated, his brain searched automatically for inspiration. 'I have some questions about the cottage and the area. I need to know where to shop, for instance. Alistair mentioned that you might help me.'

As if the mention of his brother's name reassured her, her small face cleared. She nodded, bent to bundle up one of the cats at her feet and left the room gracefully, the second cat at her heels.

Nathan waited until she'd pulled the door closed behind her before leaning back against the pillows. He expelled his breath in a long, uneasy sigh. How, he wondered, was he going to handle this?

If Libby had known he thought her graceful she would have been astounded. Her movements felt jerky and un-coordinated and her legs were clumsy as she sank gratefully onto a wooden chair in the bright sun room adjacent to Alistair's kitchen, aware that she was trembling.

Perhaps sensing her distress, the cats mewed anxiously and entwined themselves around her legs. Duncan jumped onto the table and nuzzled her but instead of putting him promptly back on the floor, as she'd normally have done, she stroked his dark fur, her thoughts distracted. It wasn't as if she'd never seen a naked man before, she told herself weakly. In fact, she'd probably seen hundreds of them.

She buried her face in Duncan's soft fur, hoping that the steady purr of her cat would transmit calming signals to her heart and help slow her racing pulse. But no matter how many bodies she'd seen, the man she could hear moving around in Nathan's bedroom had not been anything like one of her patients. He was strong and powerful and ob-viously healthy, not remotely needy or vulnerable and ab-solutely not in need of her nursing skills.

She told herself that her artist's eye had merely been captivated by the perfection of his proportions, but still it was profoundly disturbing that she could have lingered in the doorway simply watching him sleep, for so long that

William had finally grown impatient and decided to wake him.

'Tea, Libby?'

Libby jumped when he interrupted her agitated thoughts. She remembered his suggestion that she prepare drinks, but more worrying than her forgetfulness was the realisation that fully clothed, worn blue jeans and a cream jumper concealing the powerful body which had mesmerised her, he looked no less devastatingly attractive than he had when he'd been naked.

And while he didn't possess the bland, conventional good looks of Alistair, his face was harder and infinitely more compelling. She averted her gaze quickly lest his grey-blue eyes proved as all-observing as they seemed to her to be, but not before she'd registered his narrowed scrutiny of her and the promise of self-mocking good humour evident in the lifting curve of his mouth.

She'd never wanted to paint Alistair, but if she'd been brave enough she'd have asked this man to sit for her. But, of course, she wasn't brave enough and she knew she'd be doing her sketches from memory.

'Thank you, yes,' she murmured unevenly, answering his question about a drink. The tea would give her something to do with her hands, hands she now clamped firmly around Duncan, ignoring his faint mew of protest as she lifted him onto her lap. 'Alistair keeps his teas in the cupboard above the sink.' She hesitated and then, deciding he hardly looked the type to enjoy the fragrant herbal brews she and Alistair often shared, added, 'There should be coffee in the freezer.'

Confirming her assumption, he opened the little freezer atop Alistair's fridge and lifted out the jar of coffee. When he straightened again his eyes had narrowed appraisingly. 'You know your way around here.'

There was a question in the statement and Libby felt unsure. 'I own the only other cottage on this side of the bay,' she said cautiously. 'Alistair and I know each other quite well.'

'Well?'

She tucked her feet primly under the chair. 'We're good friends,' she confirmed. 'Alistair's a wonderful neighbour.'

'I'm sure.' His tone was harder now and she caught her lip nervously, relieved when he turned away and opened the tea cupboard to reveal the enormous selection Alistair kept. For a few seconds he looked taken aback, as if startled by the range, and there was a rasp of amusement in his voice when he asked, 'Any particular sort?'

'Elderflower,' she decided, in need of something to calm her nerves. As she watched him sort through the packets, she realised he hadn't even bothered to ask if she'd prefer coffee. She didn't drink it, but the thought that he'd been able to calculate her preference with the same ease with which she'd guessed his was disturbing.

'So, Libby, how long have you known Alistair?'

William had twined himself around Nathan's ankles, forcing him to step over the cat as he walked to the tap to fill the kettle. Although Libby called the animal over to her, he ignored the command, continuing to nudge against Alistair's friend until finally he bent and rubbed the cat.

'We met the day he first came to see the cottage.' She could hear William's loud purrs as the man's long fingers caressed his fur. 'That must be about two years ago now.'

'Have you lived next door long?'

'On and off for most of my life,' she told him. She suspected his questions stemmed from politeness rather than genuine curiosity, but, still, she appreciated his efforts as she felt almost tongue-tied herself. 'I more or less grew up there. The cottage belonged to my grandmother until she died.' The part about growing up in the cottage wasn't strictly true. She hadn't lived there as much as she'd wanted to because her grandmother, determined to raise Libby the way she thought her parents would have wanted, had sent her away to boarding school. However, the explanation was complicated and until she'd gone away to school and during her holidays she'd hardly left the cottage and its surrounds. And since her grandmother's death she'd lived there permanently.

She felt the movement of his gaze across her face. 'Your accent is very soft. A faint burr, nothing more.'

'I was born in London,' she admitted. 'I've spent quite a lot of time there over the years.'

She managed a nervous smile when he passed her one of Alistair's colourful mugs and the filled teapot. He pulled out the other chair from beneath the broad oak table and sat beside her. For a few minutes they sipped their drinks quietly, then he spoke, his voice low and very deep, carefully deliberate as if he'd been planning what he wanted to say, although when she heard his words she didn't understand why he would have been. 'Alistair's work must mean he's away a lot.'

The observation puzzled her and when she didn't comment he continued, his unusual dark grey-blue eyes holding her gaze far longer than felt comfortable. 'That must make things difficult.'

'Difficult?'

'For you.'

Her mouth was suddenly dry and she moistened her lower lip, catching her breath as his eyes released hers and dropped to follow the tiny movement.

'Don't you get lonely?'

The air between them seemed to have tightened somehow and that flustered her. She straightened awkwardly in her chair and Duncan, disturbed, sent her a reproachful look and leapt from her lap to the floor, landing with a soft thud. She took a hurried mouthful of her drink, watching her cat lick his brother's ear, his movements precise and affectionate. 'I have the cottage and the sea, the cats and my work,' she said finally, keeping her eyes fixed on her pets rather than on the disturbing intentness of his regard. 'I'm kept very busy.'

'You work from home?'

'Mmm.' She wished she possessed the confidence and sophistication to chat normally with this man and meet his eyes fearlessly. But she didn't. Not any longer. She'd had boyfriends in the past, casual friendships with boys, but not since coming back to Cornwall. She was…out of practice. Her life at the cottage was isolated. Apart from an occasional shopping trip into Penzance or Truro she rarely ventured out, and for the last two years the only men she'd had any social contact with, apart from Alistair, had been the mostly elderly husbands of her clients.

Even when she'd been in London she hadn't been used to dealing with men like this one. Men who were unreadable and alien. Men who wore their masculinity with easy grace and who made her overwhelmingly aware of her femininity simply by looking at her in the curiously intent way he was looking at her now. She was floundering in front of him, she knew that, and because she was a grown woman that realisation made her feel silly and embarrassed.

'You said you had some questions about the cottage,' she said stiffly, pretending to brush cat hairs from her lap. 'And about shopping.'

'Did I?'

She looked up again but his narrowed regard was still unnerving and she shifted in the chair, unaware of the smock riding up her smooth thighs until his eyes dropped to her legs. She tugged the fabric down and rushed on nervously, 'You said that Alistair told you I'd help with your questions.'

There was another brief silence then he sighed and moved back in his chair abruptly, as if he'd suddenly tired of the disturbing, half-flirtatious game he seemed to have been playing with her. 'It wasn't anything important,' he said, his tone bordering on the weary now so that she felt a pang of sick dismay as she realised that he must be finding her nervousness tiresome.

Confirming her suspicions, he stood up, pushing his cup away so that it made a scraping noise across the table. 'I'm keeping you from your work.'

'That's all right.' But it was clear she was being dismissed. She lifted her hands, bunched the heavy weight of her hair off her shoulder and let it fall down her back, then gathered Duncan up again, knowing William would follow. She walked towards the door the man had opened. 'I don't mind.'

'Then perhaps you should.' At her puzzled look he sent her an almost rueful smile, the movement demonstrating both a perfect set of white teeth and the fine creases beneath his eyes which until then she hadn't noticed. Creases that she discovered added rather than detracted from the powerful appeal of his masculinity. 'How old are you, Libby?' he asked evenly. 'Eighteen? Nineteen?'

She felt herself flushing again and understood that her colour probably only reinforced his impression that she was still a teenager. 'Twenty-four,' she corrected huskily, registering the sudden expression in his eyes which suggested he doubted her claim. 'Truly. I am. I can show you my birth certificate if you don't believe me.'

He was definitely amused now. 'That won't be necessary,' he said lazily. He held the door wide for her and watched her as she walked awkwardly past him into the sunshine, her body stiff with tension. He looked towards where the stone wall and slate roof of her cottage were just visible above the hedge which separated the properties. 'And twenty-four is still very young. Is this where you live?'

'It is.' She took a few steps, then turned, calling William away from where he was standing beside the man. Unusually for him, William didn't respond, and after a few seconds the man bent, picked up the cat and carried him back to her.

'Run away home, cat,' he said roughly, delivering the animal into Libby's waiting arm. 'Like your mistress.'

Nathan knew that he wasn't playing fair by watching Libby as she walked away from him but, knowing that, it still didn't make him look away. The graceful movements of her legs and the gentle lifting of her buttocks beneath her dress were too powerfully compelling for that. But when she finally disappeared into a gap in the hedge he sighed heavily then turned reluctantly back to Alistair's cottage.

The fact that Alistair's Libby had appeared in front of him naked, apart from the thin garment which the sun flooding into Alistair's kitchen had turned transparent, was no excuse for leering after her like some sort of sex-obsessed adolescent, he told himself wearily.

That he'd been able to see every line of her body meant nothing for, despite the garment and her nude swim the night before and no matter that she was several years older than she looked and, he'd sensed, as gratifyingly aware of him as he'd been of her, in their entire encounter she'd not sent him one remotely knowing or provocative look or gesture.

And if they'd been there he'd have noticed. Considering he hadn't been able to take his eyes off her. While her innocence puzzled him, it didn't change his confidence that the love his brother had declared had not yet been expressed physically.

He put the cups they'd used into the sink, added water and detergent, then scrubbed at the stain his coffee had left, guessing that the reason for Alistair's restraint had to be that he intended making their relationship a permanent one.

The thought wasn't an entirely…pleasant one, he conceded, upturning the washed cups onto Alistair's draining rack. The idea of spending the next *decade* or two lusting after his younger brother's wife didn't strike him as a particularly fun way of livening up family get-togethers.

Leaving the dishes to drain, he made a half-hearted attempt to sit in front of his laptop, but after a few hours he gave up and shut the lid in exasperation, resigned to the fact that he probably wasn't going to be able to achieve anything useful on his first day.

He changed into his running gear and headed outside, going first towards the edge of the cliff. He squatted there, stretching his calf muscles as he stared at the waves frothing against the dark rocks far below him.

It wasn't as if he had the excuse of abstinence to explain his reaction to his brother's girlfriend, he reflected dryly, glancing briefly behind him towards the roof of her cottage above the hedge. His work was always his priority but when he desired feminine company he had access to it. And Paula had been persistent recently. While his relationship with the anaesthetist might be based more on mutual convenience than any romantic feelings, it did at least provide an outlet for his physical needs.

Rising slowly, he stretched his quads, before setting out at a fast pace along what he could see were the faint markings of a path along the top of the cliffs.

He should be grateful for Alistair's words the previous day, he decided. Without them, instead of staring blankly at his computer screen, he'd have spent the morning contemplating the seduction of his delicious young neighbour. And that, he told himself lazily, would have been a very bad idea.

CHAPTER THREE

FANCY suggesting he check her birth certificate. Libby trudged miserably back through the hedge after her encounter with Alistair's friend. He had to think she was an absolute idiot. She released the cats and sat on her step, looking broodingly towards the cliffs and further to the sea.

William strolled over to her and promptly collapsed onto his side, paws curled, rolling over, and she stroked his luxuriant tummy fur absently.

The whole interlude had been a disaster, she reflected. No observer would have guessed she'd once been in temporary charge of a busy London hospital ward, for whatever social skills she'd once possessed seemed to have evaporated. She'd stammered and blushed her way through their conversation like some sort of witless child, and at the end of it still had no idea who he was or how long he'd be staying.

All she did know for sure was that the narrowed, faintly speculative gleam she'd caught in his eyes before she'd turned and left him had been enough to make her heart slam against her chest as if she'd been running a marathon rather than simply holding a conversation.

Brushing her hand aside, William sprang up again then skipped up the steps behind her into the cottage. He looked out at her pointedly from the kitchen as if to remind her she'd wasted enough time, and with a soft sigh she acknowledged that he was definitely right.

After restocking her workroom with fresh towels and sheets, she lingered in the doorway, relieved that the morning's upheaval had not dulled the small thrill of pride she always experienced when she inspected the neat little room.

In her grandmother's day the room had been a dark, mysterious little place, a haven of coloured bottles and strange smells. Libby's time away and her nursing training had made her infinitely more practical, and after her grandmother's death, once her immediate grief had subsided, she'd cleaned out the cobwebs, thrown away mixtures she judged ineffectual, and had had the room remodelled to the airy, open one she was looking at now.

Nevertheless, the magic of her grandmother's legacy lingered there among the books and herbs, and no matter how scientific her methods it was that magic that lent such joy to her work, a special joy she'd never experienced in her years of training within the health service.

'I'm very happy now,' she told William firmly, meeting his cool stare resolutely.

He blinked doubtfully and she frowned. 'Happy enough,' she added carefully.

Genevieve Tregoning startled her out of her thoughts by appearing in the hallway. 'Libby, dear,' she said softly. 'I did knock.'

Libby blinked, then smiled apologetically, lifting a hand to direct her client into the office. 'Sorry. Come in. I've been dreaming.'

'Not very happily,' Genevieve said shrewdly, handing her a large bag of sweetly fragrant strawberries which Libby knew would have come from her garden. 'You look worried.'

'Nonsense.' Libby dismissed the observation firmly, smiling her thanks for the fruit as she put the bag to one side. 'What in the world could I possibly be worried about, living here in paradise?' She waited for her client to lie down on the high couch, then carefully arranged the pillow so it gave extra support for her neck. 'How have you been?'

'Much better,' Genevieve told her. She lifted her hands to her carefully arranged grey hair. 'The squeezing pain is completely gone now and all I've had this week is an occasional aching at the end of the day. I saw Geoffrey yesterday and he was thrilled. But he thought I should continue perhaps with one session a fortnight, something like that. What do you think?'

Libby nodded and said, 'That sounds fine.' Geoffrey Gates, Genevieve's GP, had telephoned her the day before and mentioned the idea. Genevieve had been having almost daily tension headaches for years which he'd been unable to control. She'd resisted the idea of seeing a psychiatrist and when Geoffrey had finally referred her to Libby he'd been amazed by how quickly her headaches had improved.

She sensed that privately Geoffrey felt it was the fact that Genevieve spent an hour with her each week, discussing her troubles, which had cured her pain. While they hadn't talked about it, Libby partially agreed with the doctor's thoughts, although she was confident the infusions and massage had contributed significantly.

Genevieve herself preferred to think that it was entirely the massages and infusions and the skullcap which had freed her from pain, and for the moment, until some of her confidence and enjoyment of life returned, Libby was happy to leave it at that. They chatted quietly while Libby gently prepared and then blended a mix of rosemary and lavender, diluted with oil from crushed apricot kernels, then she covered her client's hair and clothes with towels and tipped her head back.

'How's Ray?' she asked gently, anointing her fingers.

Genevieve sighed, closing her eyes as Libby began softly massaging her temples. 'A little brighter this week,' she said, her voice calmer now than it used to be when she discussed her husband. 'He's going for respite care next week. When he remembers I get the impression he's quite looking forward to it.'

Libby's fingers slid to Genevieve's cheeks. 'And you?' she asked softly, knowing that the two weeks Ray spent in care every few months was normally a difficult time for her, a time she spent rocking between relief that she was free of the burden of caring for him and guilt that she should feel such relief.

'I thought I might join that class you suggested,' Genevieve said. 'The painting one. They're running a residential course in St Ives the first week Ray's away, and if I want to continue Geoffrey can arrange for someone to call in and watch him one evening a week.'

'Good.' Libby smiled. It was the first time she'd heard Genevieve actively plan to do something just for herself. 'And Marie?'

'I'm going to visit her in the second week,' Genevieve said. 'I haven't been to London in years—it'll be a good break.'

'Perhaps she'll want to come back with you?'

'I don't think so, dear.' But Genevieve sounded remarkably philosophical. 'It's hard for her. She wants the father she grew up with, not someone who doesn't remember her name.' She let Libby tip her head to one side. 'She wants me to put him in a home,' she added, mentioning for the first time something which Libby had sensed had been worrying her.

'She's thinking of you,' Libby said softly.

'I *want* to care for him,' Genevieve said firmly, as if she'd finally come to some sort of definite understanding about it. 'I'm not just doing my duty.'

After Libby had finished the massage and consultation, Genevieve mentioned the subject again. 'I do understand it's stress that's been causing the headaches,' she said, hesitating in the doorway. 'These past few years haven't been easy, but even though Alzheimer's has changed Ray so much, underneath he's still the man I loved, Libby, and I loved him *desperately*. You can't just switch off something like that or forget it.'

Libby stood at the gate, watching until the car disappeared around the curve in the lane, disturbed by the glimpse of the powerful emotions behind Genevieve's gentle worried eyes. She'd loved Ray 'desperately', she'd said. *Desperately*. Such an evocative word. It implied urgency and passion and overwhelming need. An intensity of love which drove her now to devote herself to a man who even on his best days no longer recognised her.

Absently Libby changed the sheets and collected the used linen, carrying it through into her kitchen. She bundled them into the washing-machine, closed the door, then hesitated, staring out of the window and across towards the roof of Alistair's cottage. 'I loved him *desperately*,' she said experimentally, trying out Genevieve's words. '*Desperately*.'

The washing started, she found herself too restless to stay in the cottage, waiting for the cycle to finish. She left a note on her front door in case any of her clients called, saying that she was swimming and could be called from the cliff, then ran down to the beach.

William and Duncan disliked sea water and they sat on her towel, watching her balefully as she dived into the water and swam strongly out against the incoming tide. About a hundred yards out, she stopped, then flipped, treading water, her hair floating on the waves like a veil surrounding her as she looked back at the cottage. So small and high, from here it could have been a child's play hut.

Her gaze drifted to the cottage next door and she saw a dark figure above the cliff. Her breath caught in her throat. Alistair's friend was watching her. For a few seconds she lingered there, flushing, feeling as if their eyes were locked together even though she was too far away to make out his face.

Then he moved and the spell broke. He was moving back towards the cottage and within seconds she couldn't see him any more.

Abruptly she kicked forward, all enjoyment of her swim drained for some reason. She swam quickly towards her waiting cats, pausing only to wipe her face dry before making for the path with Duncan already halfway up, William at her heels. When she reached the top Alistair's friend appeared a few yards ahead of her. To her surprise he was walking swiftly away from her cottage as if he'd visited for some reason and was now in a hurry to return home.

She froze, and then he saw her and stopped also, his expression entirely neutral and not at all surprised. 'I've returned your broom,' he said calmly. 'It's beside your door there. You left it in Alistair's kitchen.'

'Thank you.' She mopped her forehead with a towel, catching some of the water that was dripping from her hair. It occurred to her that he'd deliberately chosen to return the broom at that moment because he'd known she was swimming, and had wanted to avoid her. The thought hurt but she still found herself trying to delay his departure. 'I've been for a swim,' she blurted out.

'So I see.' His eyes flickered to her damp swimsuited figure but almost immediately returned to her face. 'The water must have been cold. The sun's warm but you're still covered in goose bumps.'

'It wasn't as cold as it can be at this time of year.' She shifted her weight between her two bare feet, letting the towel fall open so it concealed her, self-conscious although her suit was modest. 'It's very refreshing. You should try it,' she said awkwardly. 'Swimming, that is. If you like it.'

'I may.' The corners of his mouth lifted and she realised that she'd amused him again. 'One day.'

'Well, if you want company, just call out.' She felt rather brave, saying that and meeting his enigmatic regard at the same time. 'Alistair and I often swim together when he's here. Please, don't think you'll be disturbing me by asking. I love swimming and I'd be happy to show you the beach.'

His brows lifted slightly but, instead of answering, he said merely, 'Your hair's very long.'

'It's easy to look after that way.' She lifted a self-conscious hand to smooth away the few errant strands which had drifted across her face. 'It's quite fine. It doesn't take long to dry.'

'And it's very obvious you love swimming. You're good.'

'Apparently my father used to call me his little mermaid.' Her lashes fluttered down and she felt her face colour from his acknowledgement that he'd been watching her in the water. 'He taught me to swim when I was a baby.'

'Apparently?'

'My parents died when I was very young,' she explained. 'I barely remember them,' she added quickly, to stem the flow of platitudes that admission usually engendered.

But Alistair's friend didn't offer any platitudes. Instead, he took a quiet step towards her, held out one long finger and tilted her chin, meaning she had to meet his blue-grey assessment again if she weren't to risk appearing embarrassingly coy. 'And your grandmother?'

She recalled mentioning her grandmother to him earlier and the fact that he'd remembered gave her an unexpected flicker of pleasure. 'She died almost two years ago.'

'Brothers and sisters?'

Libby lifted her chin free of his finger and without quibble he released her. 'I was an only child.'

'So now you're all alone.'

'I'm an adult,' she told him quietly, looking up at him. She wasn't a short person, almost five feet six in bare feet, but while she'd always considered Alistair very tall his friend was taller. 'I'm fully grown,' she added huskily. 'Hardly abandoned.'

'And, of course, you have Alistair.' Her brows knitted but he didn't give her a chance to question that because he'd stepped back, his expression utterly inscrutable. 'But Alistair's away, isn't he?' he said evenly. 'So there's nobody to protect you.'

'I don't need protection,' she countered stiffly, not understanding why her declaration should have provoked the brief amusement that flashed across his face. 'I'm quite capable of looking after myself.'

'I wonder,' he murmured. Then he was turning away from her. 'To protect yourself you first need to understand what you need to protect yourself from. Have a care, Libby.' He left her and she stood very still, watching his back with a puzzled frown until he disappeared into Alistair's.

Nathan went straight to Alistair's fridge, extracted a lager, opened it and took a long mouthful. He wiped his mouth then threw himself into one of the rocking chairs in Alistair's sun room. He propped his feet on the coffee-table, tipped himself back and let his eyes close.

Libby's hair had hung like wet silk across her shoulders and he'd wanted to wrap them both in it and bind her to him. The impulse had been disconcerting. He wasn't used to experiencing…primitive emotions. Certainly not repeatedly. And certainly not towards a woman who was entirely unsuitable if not actually forbidden.

Yes, he'd been able to walk away without making either a fool of himself or potentially destroying his relationship with Alistair, but it hadn't been easy.

His mouth curving in a mixture of exasperation and self-disgust, he finished his beer, crushed the can in his fist and reached for the telephone. His second day into his holiday and he was already going mad. If he was needed at the hospital, at that moment he was willing, more than willing, to get in his car now and drive straight up. He punched out the numbers for the hospital. Minutes later the switchboard was putting him through to his registrar. 'Richard? Nathan. How are our chaps with the aneurysms?'

'Fine.' Richard sounded amused. Given that his registrar had once labelled him a workaholic, Nathan guessed he'd been expecting his call. 'Forgotten you're supposed to be on leave, boss?'

Nathan ignored that. 'Legs all right?'

'No problems. The emergency chap's still missing a pulse on the left but we knew that anyway. The foot's warm and healthy and we can pick up the pulse on ultrasound. It'll be all right.'

'No other emergencies?'

Richard laughed. 'Settle down. Sounds like you're touting for work.'

'You're saying there isn't any?'

'Not a scrap. Relax. Enjoy your break. You deserve it. We'll cope.'

But would he? Grimacing as he hung up, Nathan redialled the hospital. Ignoring his misgivings, he had the switchboard bleep Paula.

She, at least, sounded pleased to hear from him. 'Darling,' she said happily. 'I was hoping you'd call. I'm busy but luckily you've caught me between cases. Actually, there's something rather…delicate that I wanted to talk to you about. How's Cornwall?'

'Fine. Paula…?'

'It's just my period, darling. It's probably nothing to worry about but it's just the teeniest, weeniest bit late.' She stopped, and when he didn't say anything she rushed on, 'I forgot to tell you at the time but the last time we…well,

I forgot my diaphragm, darling. I didn't think it would matter just the once.'

Nathan closed his eyes. 'How late?'

'A week.'

'Have you done a test?'

'I thought I'd wait a little longer,' she told him. 'I've never been regular and even if it was positive these things don't always last at such an early stage.'

He frowned. He knew he'd have preferred to have known immediately one way or the other but he conceded that he had no right to ask that of her. 'I'll drive up tomorrow.'

'Nathan!' She sounded taken aback. 'How sweet. But, darling, there's no point. I've a full-day list tomorrow and I'm on call all this week and next and my sister's bringing her ghastly children to stay for some awful show and I'll have to cart them about the place. You being here won't make the slightest difference to anything, and frankly I don't even think I'd have time to see you. I'd rather you stayed where you were. London's stuffy at the moment so I'd love to come away for a few days next week. How about inviting me to visit you for a long weekend?'

'Cornwall's too far for you to drive when you could be pregnant,' he countered, frowning. 'And you shouldn't be working so many hours. Can you take time off?'

'I don't want to, silly.' Her laugh floated down the line. 'Even if I am *with child*, it doesn't make me an invalid. I'm as fit as a fiddle. I haven't had a chance to take the new car for a decent spin yet so a long drive will be fun. Don't you dare come up and spoil that for me. Besides, it's not as if either of us actually *wants* a baby, is it?'

Nathan's fingers curled around the receiver so hard they hurt. 'You tell me,' he said carefully. 'Isn't it more that neither of us has discussed the possibility before?'

Perhaps sensing his seriousness and unwilling to confront it, she came back quickly and frustratingly with, 'I'll be down next weekend. Now, don't argue because I won't listen to you. We'll talk about things then, darling. Fax me directions. They're bleeping me now for my next case. Have to rush. Bye, darling. Bye.'

Nathan put the receiver carefully back onto its cradle and then stared at it for a few minutes. Softly, under his breath, he swore.

Later, after a couple more beers and a few generous splashes of Alistair's best Scotch, he decided Paula's news wasn't so bad. And her throw-away comment about not wanting the baby, if she did turn out to be pregnant, wasn't to be taken seriously because it had come before he'd had a chance to tell her that naturally, if there was to be a baby, he would want them to formalise their relationship with marriage.

He lifted one leg over the arm of his chair. He enjoyed the company of his young nieces and nephews and he'd always assumed he would at some stage have children of his own. Paula was an attractive woman. His body might not react to her as violently or…inconveniently as it was reacting at the moment to Alistair's young neighbour, but, then, it hadn't done that for any other woman either. Broadly speaking, he and Paula were sexually compatible. Also he respected her dedication to her career. She was the best anaesthetist he'd ever worked with.

He tipped back his glass and then poured himself another measure. She understood the hours he had to work. Their liaison had been convenient for both of them and he had no reason to think she'd object to it becoming permanent.

He swallowed the whisky in two long gulps and dumped the glass heavily onto the table. That was it, then. They would be a good partnership.

Which had the convenient advantage of neatly disposing

of any risk of him being tempted into an involvement with Alistair's luscious Libby, he acknowledged, studying his empty glass thoughtfully. From now on he had to consider himself an engaged man.

CHAPTER FOUR

Two days later, Monica Mulholland, Libby's second client of the morning, rushed into the cottage a few minutes late for her appointment, her lively blue eyes wide with curiosity. 'I've just seen the most incredible man,' she said breathlessly as she took off her coat and handed it, along with an enormous bag of meat for the cats, to Libby to put away. 'He drove up behind me in the lane. Black Saab convertible. Dark hair. Tall. So-o good-looking. Is he coming to see you?'

Libby only knew one man who deserved the word 'incredible'. Her nerves jerked. 'Probably Alistair's friend,' she said huskily. She hadn't seen him at all the day before and when his car hadn't been there that morning she'd wondered if he'd left.

Ignoring the surge of excitement Monica's words had provoked, she said merely, 'He's been staying at Alistair's, but I haven't seen him for a few days.'

Monica whistled. 'Perhaps I'll call in,' she said airily from behind the screen as she changed into one of the towelling robes Libby had left out. She peeked out. 'Borrow some sugar.'

Libby forced a smile. 'Your husband might have something to say about that.'

'Oh, him!' Monica waved a dismissive hand, but the twinkle in her eye as she climbed onto the couch showed she was joking. 'Problem is four teenagers and stretch marks,' she joked. 'Together they might dampen the poor man's ardour a little.' She wiggled into a comfortable position. 'Tell you what, though,' she continued. 'If I were

40

ten years younger…' She laughed. 'Well, maybe twenty,' she admitted with a wry shrug. 'Men like that were never in my league anyway.' She tilted her head back, eyeing Libby speculatively. 'Now, you, Libby. You're quite gorgeous. You could have any man you—'

'No. I couldn't.' Flushing, Libby found her hand lifting to stop Monica's words before she could finish. 'And even if I could, I wouldn't want to,' she said firmly. 'That's not me. I like the peaceful life.'

Quickly she rubbed some oil between her palms to warm it then she rested calming hands on her client's shoulders. 'I've added camomile to the geranium oil today,' she said quietly, feeling the tension beginning to drain out of Monica's deltoid muscles. 'How's the peppermint going?'

'The hot flushes have eased off,' her client told her languidly. 'Also, whatever's in that stuff you've given me for my baths is working wonders. I feel like a new woman after them. I'm even getting my interest in you-know-what back again. Rex is over the moon.'

Libby smiled. 'I'm glad.' The mixture of herbs Monica was using was designed to help her body increase production of its own natural oestrogen. Monica had been unable to tolerate conventional hormone replacement therapy and had come along to Libby because she'd been interested in finding out about herbal alternatives. 'I'm glad they're helping.'

After Libby had finished the massage and Monica had had time to recover and dress, she again mentioned the subject Libby had been hoping to avoid. 'Is there anyone with this man?' she asked lightly. 'Is he involved, do you think? Girlfriend, wife…?'

'I have no idea,' Libby told her, equally casually. But she was glad she had the excuse of tidying her oils to keep her eyes averted because the question was disturbing. He'd been alone but that didn't mean he was single, and while he hadn't worn a ring, not all men did. 'Anything's possible.'

She escorted Monica out to her car but instead of driving away immediately the older woman wound down her window. 'You know that love potion you gave to Melissa really did the trick,' she called. 'He proposed last week.'

'It wasn't a love potion,' Libby scolded. 'It was a fragrance. A gift, nothing more.'

'You don't fool me, Libby Deane.' Monica's eyes flashed. 'Your grandmother gave me exactly the same gift when I was courting.' She leaned a little out of the car. 'And it worked for me too.' She started the car, but didn't drive off. 'If I were you I'd spray it on heavily,' she advised. 'It's not healthy, a girl like you all alone.' Pointedly she shifted her gaze to the cottage next door. 'Let him get a good dose of that ''fragrance'' of yours.' She laughed, clearly unabashed by Libby's embarrassed expression. 'See you next week,' she shouted, as she accelerated away.

Her next client, together with her husband, arrived almost immediately after Monica had left, and Libby helped her from the car. 'It's been much better since Monday,' Mrs Spalding told her. 'I'm getting around a lot more.'

'Good.' Libby helped her inside, then scrubbed her hands, set up a trolley and put on some gloves before unrolling the dressing she'd left over the wound on Mrs Spalding's leg. She'd been treating the ulcer for several weeks now and initially it had been very large and sloughy, having grown from a trivial knock or bruise a year or so earlier and then stubbornly refused to heal.

Carefully Libby lifted away the pad she'd left against the defect. 'Oh, yes, that's very good,' she said, pleased with the fresh pink base of healthy granulation tissue which was a sign of healing. 'A big improvement.' She dipped a swab into some sterile saline and gently cleaned the one edge that was still a little sloughy. 'Did you see Dr Gates yesterday?'

'He was very pleased,' her client said proudly. 'You know, he'd told me my circulation was so bad that this would probably never heal. He called you a "miracle-worker".'

Libby smiled. 'He's very flattering,' she said lightly. 'Still enjoying the tea?'

'That drink's done wonders,' Mrs Spalding said flatly. 'It's what's curing me.'

Libby made a noncommittal sound but the older woman persisted. 'I've had months of dressings,' she said. 'Apart from the comfrey, you're not doing much more than what the district nurse did for me with them. The only thing that's different is the drink.' She peered over her glasses at Libby. 'You should patent that stuff,' she advised. 'You'd make a fortune.'

Libby laughed. 'It's basically only marigold leaves.' She finished the dressing and re-covered the area with a crêpe bandage. 'But I'm glad you think it's working for you.'

'You've got your grandmother's gift, child.' Mrs Spalding leaned on Libby as they walked back outside towards where her husband waited in the car, too shy to venture into the house. 'Anybody can see that.'

'It's not a gift,' Libby said firmly. 'It's a skill. A skill I've been taught. See you Tuesday.'

It was another soft, clear day and that afternoon she assembled her painting kit and set out along the cliff path to the north of the cottage. It meant walking in front of Alistair's cottage, but a quick glance at the firmly closed door and shut windows told her that if his friend was there he wasn't in the mood for casual callers.

'Thank goodness,' she said to William, but William didn't look convinced, and privately Libby wasn't surprised. She hadn't exactly convinced herself.

She walked about a mile along the curving cliffside track, climbing up to a small rocky summit before the path dived into the next bay. Slightly breathless from the exertion of carrying her equipment, she set up her easel at the top, facing down into one of the neighbouring bays. She was alone now, both William and Duncan having abandoned her long ago to go stalking insects in Alistair's garden, and for a few minutes she just rested, absorbing the scene—the water, the gulls screeching, the tiny stony beach and the long, windswept grasses of the cliff.

When she was ready to begin she sketched in the faint outlines of the picture, working fluidly and confidently at the initial stage. Once she had her proportions right she switched to concentrating on capturing the quality of the light, the way the water caught it and reflected it into a soft mist on the horizon, using the water to flood her colours and emphasise the gentle, sun-washed appearance of the beach and shoreline.

Some time later, perhaps hours later because she'd virtually finished and when she painted she lost track of time, a movement close behind her snapped her concentration. The hairs on the back of her arms stood up and she whirled around.

'You're good,' Alistair's friend said quietly.

'N-not really.' Her hair had worked itself loose in the wind and when she scrambled up it whipped across her face, blinding her. She brushed the weight of it away, then realised that several long strands had tangled in the cream wool of his jumper. Flustered, she reached to tug them away, but immediately his hand caught her wrist.

Libby gasped, for although his grip was gentle her skin quivered. Her eyes flew to his face, but he didn't meet her wide-eyed gaze, his blue-grey eyes almost thoughtful as he lifted her hair away.

Then slowly, as if it were the most natural thing in the

world, he tucked the strands carefully behind her ear, his fingers lingering for a few taut moments against her flushed cheek.

The hand that was gripping her wrist shifted slightly, almost, she thought faintly, as if he were checking her pulse. 'I've frightened you,' he murmured.

'Surprised me,' she countered shakily, knowing it wasn't him who'd frightened her. The fear had come from recognising her reaction to him. 'I didn't hear you coming.'

He dropped her hand then watched it swing loosely back to nudge her thigh. 'I didn't want to interrupt.' His mouth compressed and she had the impression he was angry with himself about something. 'But curiosity overcame my good intentions,' he finished flatly.

He crouched in front of her picture, the easy movement emphasising the strength of the thighs beneath the taut, faded denim of his jeans. 'I like this very much,' he said softly. He lifted his head, his expression unreadable. 'Do you sell your pictures?'

Libby's throat made a convulsive movement. 'Occasionally,' she admitted. 'If I think they're not too awful.'

'Sell me this.'

It was a statement, not a question, but she didn't resist and simply nodded.

'Will you finish it now?'

'There's only a little more to do.' The wind picked up one of her brushes and rolled it across the smooth wood of her carry case. She snatched it up, grateful to have something to occupy her hands. 'Give me a few hours. You could…' She hesitated, then rushed on, knowing that unless she spoke quickly her courage would evaporate. 'You could come to the cottage for supper. I'll have it ready by then.'

He stood slowly, looking down at the frothing waves, saying nothing, a solemn, abstracted air about him suggesting he hadn't registered her nervous invitation. Libby flushed, embarrassed, but wasn't brave enough to repeat her words.

Then he looked at her, his face the mask of polite regret people used to avoid unwelcome things, and she realised he'd heard every word and had merely been thinking of an excuse to avoid spending time with her. Quietly he said, 'No, Libby. I don't think so.' He looked back towards the cottage, apparently restless now, obviously keen to leave her. 'I'll be out tomorrow morning,' he added distantly. 'I'm going to drive into Truro again to pick up a few groceries. Just leave it on the porch.'

All she wanted to do was melt quietly away into the earth but she forced herself to straighten. 'OK,' she said, doing her best to make it sound casual. 'That's fine. Of course. Whatever's most convenient for you.'

He thrust his hands into the pockets of his jeans. 'Remember to leave your bill, of course.'

'I will.'

Abruptly he turned, as if to start walking back, but a few yards down the track he seemed to change his mind and stopped. Libby hadn't moved and she bravely met his gaze when he looked back at her. 'Any news from Alistair?'

'It's too soon,' she told him abruptly, wanting him to go now. It had only been a dinner invitation, she told herself thickly. She barely knew the man. What did it matter if he didn't want to eat with her? 'The mail takes weeks from places like that.'

'He hasn't called you?'

'Alistair? No.' She turned around, away from him, blinking fast. She didn't understand why he could reduce her to such a fragile state but it seemed that he could. 'He doesn't call very often.'

'Libby?' She heard his feet slide on the grassy path as he walked towards her again. 'Are you upset about Ali not getting in touch?'

She could feel him behind her and quickly she wiped her eyes with her sleeve so he wouldn't see her tears, but she didn't turn around. 'No, I'm fine,' she said firmly, feeling ridiculous and bewildered and embarrassed all at the same time. 'Really.'

He muttered something under his breath. She heard him move again but he didn't touch her. 'He's probably very busy,' he said soothingly. 'I'm sure he's thinking of you.'

She stiffened as she realised he was talking about Alistair and that he thought she was missing his friend. Then his hands touched her shoulders, rubbed the top of her arms as if to comfort her, and her senses swam, all thoughts of correcting him flying out of her head.

'Stop worrying,' he was murmuring, and she didn't question why it should feel so utterly and completely right that this man should touch her like this.

She concentrated on the way his warm, gentle hands were moving rhythmically up and down her upper arms. Despite the coolness of the wind here, the heat of him penetrated her jumper and sent tiny flickers of flame across her skin.

'Alistair likes to play things light-heartedly,' she heard him say, his voice distorted by the dull thud of her pulse in her ears, 'but underneath I promise you he's completely loyal. You can trust him.'

Libby closed her eyes, felt herself sway back against him, the knowledge that he intended only to comfort her no barrier to the involuntary response of her own body.

Distantly, vaguely, she was aware that he was still talking. 'He loves you,' he said, and although she knew it not to be true, at least not in the way he meant, she didn't protest, letting him say anything as long as he kept holding her.

'He's the sort who, once he loves, loves for life,' he said, his hands now caressing the whole length of her arms, from shoulder to fingers, slowly, repeatedly, gloriously. 'Trust me, Libby. Family and family life are both very important to him.'

He stopped then, his movements stilling so the two of them stood together quietly, her back to him, the weight of her transmitted through her head to his chest, their hands entwined.

Libby shook her head, just slightly, a tiny movement, barely noticeable, but the way his hands tightened on hers suggested he'd felt it and had misunderstood its meaning. 'Believe me,' he insisted, as if he thought her movement a denial of his words. 'I know him. I know what matters to him.'

His hands slid back to her shoulders and firmly he lifted her away, forced her to support her own weight again although her limbs seemed drained of strength. 'He does love you,' he said forcibly. 'Don't doubt that.'

Slowly, very slowly, as though this were some sort of dream and she had to fight through the mists of sleep, she managed to turn around to face him, the movement dislodging his arms so she felt at once chilled and abandoned. 'No, you've got it wrong,' she said finally. 'You don't understand. I'm not in love with Alistair. And Alistair certainly doesn't love me.'

His expression was already unreadable, but at her words it was as if shutters came down and his face smoothed into a mask of cool disinterest. 'Libby, regardless of your own feelings, if you really believe that Alistair doesn't love you then it's you who has it wrong.'

Before she could speak, ask him about that, explain properly about Alistair, he left her. Within seconds he was too far down the track to hear even if she called.

Nathan went directly from Libby back the way he'd come, then down the cliff path to the beach below the cottages, his fingers moving impatiently over the fastenings of his clothes as he descended the steep track.

He left his things on the bottom step then waded out into the sea. When the water lapped his knees he dived cleanly in, his teeth gritting as the icy water flooded over him.

It would have been so easy, he knew, powering himself through the water, long strokes propelling him far from the shore. It could be easy again. She was so completely…trusting.

He stopped abruptly, treading water as the possible consequences of that occurred to him. She was achingly vulnerable here, he realised. She had no family and there were no other neighbours. When Alistair was away, and Alistair was often away, she was completely alone. Even the police would struggle to reach the bay within thirty minutes in an emergency. What if he'd been a man with a taste for inflicting pain?

He tried to laugh at himself. He told himself his reaction was absurd, but still his blood ran cold. The feeling of wanting to protect her was unwelcome but overwhelming. He wanted to build a cordon around her, he realised faintly, disturbed by the idiocy of the urge. He wanted to turn her cottage into a fortress. He wanted to hire security guards. Alarms. Dogs. And while reason told him his fears were ludicrous, that she wasn't in any danger and that he had no right to offer any of those things, the urgent, aroused part of his brain still found the truths hard to accept.

He swam vigorously back to the shore, checking with a glance that Libby wasn't returning along the cliffs before he waded out onto the beach. He rubbed himself roughly dry with his shirt then pulled on his jeans and trainers before easing his jumper over his head, balling the damp shirt and his underwear into his fist.

He'd spend some time with Libby, he vowed as he started up the path. In an…avuncular way. He'd try and convince her to heed advice about security and he'd try and encourage her to grow a little more wary.

He didn't need to keep shutting himself away with his work. After all, he was virtually an engaged man now. He'd touched her just now, yes, but only to comfort her, and he'd been able to walk away despite knowing from the softening of her body that she wouldn't have fought him if he hadn't.

Paula's pregnancy test the day before had been negative, which meant that she was very unlikely to be pregnant although he knew neither of them would feel sure of that until her period began. He'd pointed out that they ought to marry if there was a baby and she'd agreed that that would be appropriate, so he was still, to all intents and purposes, a committed man. Libby was safe with him.

When Nathan reached the top of the path Libby was just appearing around the hedge that separated the cottages. His eyes narrowed on the faint stains in her cheeks which, he guessed, came not from the exertion of carrying her painting equipment along the cliffs but from her embarrassment as she saw him watching her.

'You're wet,' she observed shakily, and he noted how she'd slowed her approach. 'You must have been swimming.'

'You're back sooner than I was expecting.' He noted the way her gaze fluttered down as if his scrutiny embarrassed her, and he clenched his fists, fighting the urge to grasp her chin and tilt her lovely face up to him. 'Did you finish the painting?'

She was looking at the ground, at the sea, anywhere, apparently, but at him. 'It's almost done,' she revealed. 'There's only a little more to do. I'll finish it tonight and…drop it over tomorrow as we arranged.'

Nathan knew his earlier rejection was responsible for the new rush of colour to her cheeks and he felt his gut contract with stale guilt. 'Libby, I didn't mean…' But he stopped, not knowing what he could say to ease her embarrassment without risking a situation he was determined to avoid. 'When I said no to supper I didn't mean I didn't want to spend time with you,' he finished flatly.

She looked at him, as vulnerable as a kitten. 'It's all right,' she said quietly, giving the words a dignity which tugged the guilt inside him as taut as a bow. 'I may not be particularly sophisticated but I do have some sensitivity.' She straightened her shoulders. 'I didn't really expect you to want to come to supper. I expect you'd find it a boring way of spending—'

'No.' The word was out before he could stop it, before he realised that perhaps her thinking that was the best thing that could have happened. 'No. I wouldn't.' He let his damp clothes fall to the ground, allowing him to take her shoulders gently. 'I wouldn't find it boring at all,' he heard himself insisting. 'I don't find you boring, Libby. On the contrary, I find you…entirely delightful.'

Increasing his self-disgust immeasurably, she let her head rest trustingly on his chest, her body relaxing against him as his arms folded involuntarily around her. 'I'm sorry,' she said thickly, her sweet voice muffled against his jumper. 'I barely know you. It shouldn't matter one scrap to me what you think of me, but for some reason…it does seem to.'

He closed his eyes weakly, absorbing her scent, taking care to hold his lower body away from her, sickened that the embrace he'd intended to be soothing was arousing him so utterly.

A few minutes later she lifted her head, her green eyes soft and misted. 'I'm not usually this…pathetic,' she whispered. 'Please, don't think I always behave so idiotically.'

He brushed her cheek with the pad of his thumb. 'You're

very young.' He reminded himself forcefully that he didn't mean just in years.

Her teeth bit softly into her lower lip and the small gesture made his pulse surge. When she spoke her voice was strained, strained and enticingly husky, like syrup against his skin. 'Am I too young for you?'

He doubted she knew what she was saying. 'Far too young,' he observed dryly, some of his good humour restored by the sweet naïvety of her demand.

She took a deep breath and he felt the firm, rising pressure of her breasts against his chest. Immediately he pushed her back, uncomfortably aware that, despite his fine words and equally fine possible engagement, unless he got her away from him his hands might slide beneath her clothes.

'Forgive me again,' she repeated distantly, straightening the pale jumper which had ridden a little up on her slender hips. 'I have made a fool of myself today. You shouldn't worry that it's going to happen again. I promise I'll keep my distance in future.'

He gathered his clothes, and then, scarcely able to believe he was opening himself up to such punishment, he heard himself say, 'Libby, I was wrong before. I shouldn't have been impolite when you invited me to supper. If the invitation's still open I would like to come.'

Her eyelids came down, but he saw the small lifting of her throat as she swallowed. 'Of course it's still open.' She raised her eyes and he saw that a little of her embarrassment had faded. He felt a surge of pleasure that at least he'd been able to do that. At what cost to himself, he refused to consider. 'I'd like that.' She bit her lip again and he had to fight the urge to stop her, to soothe her imprisoned lip, to cover it with his mouth. 'Eight-thirty?'

He checked his watch. It was only seven. He had time to get himself together. 'Eight-thirty,' he agreed.

She smiled, a sweet, open, carefree smile, and it felt to him as if the sun had suddenly emerged from the clouds.

Back at the cottage he showered away the salt which still clung to his skin from the sea then grimaced at his reflection in the mirror above the basin. He looked like a tramp, he thought, running a rueful hand over the dark stubble which had roughened his skin since he'd shaved early that morning.

He had a sudden vision of Libby, her long, pale throat reddened from the rasp of his face, and he reached for his razor. He grimaced as he realised what he was doing and put it carefully back onto the shelf, deliberately leaving his skin rough. He was going for supper. Supper, he told himself wearily. Despite his behaviour today, he wasn't an idiot. He couldn't and he wouldn't let himself touch her again.

A towel carelessly slung around his waist, he padded into the sun room and leaned against the wall, staring broodingly at the remains of Alistair's whisky. The temptation was there but not strongly enough to overcome his good sense, he acknowledged finally, leaving the alcohol untouched.

Deliberately he shifted his attention to the laptop that taunted him from the opposite corner of the room. In three days he'd achieved practically nothing as far as his work was concerned. Starting now, that was going to change. Libby wasn't expecting him for over an hour. He had time to finish indexing, he calculated.

But shortly before it would have been time to dress and leave, his vision shifted. He lifted his eyes from the screen and stared at the wall in front of him, then lifted a hand to the side of his head and groaned, recognising the sudden haziness in the centre of his vision and the first dull throb of pain at his temple.

Understanding what was going to happen within the next

few minutes, he realised he had to reach Libby. Before he lost his vision entirely. He'd already hurt her today by his thoughtlessness. He couldn't let her think he simply hadn't bothered to come.

CHAPTER FIVE

LIBBY was putting the vegetables she'd prepared into the oven when Alistair's friend appeared in her doorway, naked apart from a bath towel knotted low on his hips. She straightened, his pallor and the strained lines of his face distracting her eyes from the strength of his body. 'Is something…wrong?'

'Migraine.' He stumbled into the room and grabbed one of her chairs as if to support himself. 'Sorry,' he muttered, shielding his eyes with one of his hands. 'I haven't had one in years.'

She moved quickly to switch off the lights, the evening glow from outside more than enough to help her guide him into the chair properly. 'There's a bowl here,' she told him, sliding the large bowl she'd been about to use to prepare dessert towards him. 'Are you going to be sick?'

'Not yet,' he said hoarsely, but then he grabbed for the bowl and promptly threw up. 'Hell!' he muttered. 'Sorry.'

'I don't mind.' She swapped the bowl for another one, then carried the used one into her bathroom and returned a few minutes later, paling when she saw how unwell he looked now. He lowered his head onto his hands and she could see that the muscles of his back had gone taut with pain. 'Have you any tablets?'

'Nothing. It's been too long. I thought I was over them.'

She walked across to him, stroked the back of his neck and felt the cold moistness of his sweat beneath her fingers. 'I'll call a doctor.'

'No.' He tried to lift his head but the movement must have been agonising because he immediately lowered it again. 'I don't need a doctor,' he said. 'Too late, anyway. I have to sleep it off. It could take days.' His words were slightly slurred but his feet shifted as if he wanted to move. 'I have to get back to Alistair's.'

'Stay here,' she urged, worried. 'I'll look after you.'

'No.' He shook his head, then groaned again. 'I have to get back.'

'You can't leave.' She rested her hand on his neck, feeling his pain, wishing she could will it away. 'You can hardly see,' she added calmly. 'You'll fall over the cliff.'

His shoulders sagged as if he recognised the truth of that and then urgently he reached for the bowl again.

When he'd finished she took the bowl away and cleaned it, then helped him along the hall to her room and into her bed. She pulled up the covers, added another blanket because he felt cold and crouched beside him. 'Do you get mouth ulcers?'

He frowned, his mouth twisting as if he thought the question stupid, but was obviously too weakened by pain to resist her. 'Never.'

She rested the back of her hand on his forehead, checking his temperature, and that, too, was cool. 'Back soon,' she said softly, guiding one of his hands to the bowl so he could feel where it was if he needed it again.

He was still awake when she returned, his eyes squeezed shut, his brow wrinkled with pain. 'Sit up for me,' she said gently. 'Just for a moment, then you can sleep.'

He let her help him up slowly, opened his eyes a fraction and half scowled at the sandwich she offered him. 'I can't eat,' he protested, obviously not so weak he'd let her do anything.

'You have to,' she insisted. Carefully she explained that hunger might be making his headache worse and that the sandwich contained something that would help him.

His mouth compressed but when she tore off a piece of

the bread and held it to his mouth he relented, chewing with a slow wariness that made her heart ache for him.

She supported him until he'd finished then helped him settle back down, pressing the warm compress she'd prepared to his forehead. Her fingers longed to caress him, to try and soothe away his pain, but she knew he was too ill. She worried that her touch would be an intrusion, not an aid. 'Try to sleep,' she said softly. 'I'll be here if you need anything.'

He wasn't sick again, and after about eleven he became less restless, his dozing gradually easing into sleep. She brought oils she could use to massage him if he still couldn't sleep once his pain had eased slightly, but put them aside once she realised they wouldn't be needed. She checked on him several times after that, changing his compress every few hours and grabbing snatches of sleep on the couch in her workroom in between times.

When Libby rose at nine he was still asleep. He lay on his front, his hands splayed either side of her pillow, his head turned away, his strong legs sprawled apart with his left knee bent up. Some time since she'd last seen him he'd dislodged the blankets and now he was covered only by the sheet, which had slid to his hips.

Libby crouched beside him and touched his shoulder to assess his temperature, relieved to find he'd warmed up again.

Instead of lifting her hand away, she found herself watching helplessly as it slid across his back, all pretence of treating him as if he were one of her patients evaporating as she acknowledged the rapid acceleration of her pulse. His back was warm and smooth and the texture of him gave her pleasure.

Her mouth dried. Telling herself that this was for him, not her, she forced her hands away long enough to blend her oils and coat her palms, but when she came back to him the warmth that flooded her proved that wrong.

She tried to swallow, but the movement seemed too complicated. Instead, her whole being was concentrated on the impulses from the palm that seemed somehow dissociated from her as it glided towards his hips, nudging the edge of the sheet before it slid back up towards his shoulder.

Her movements were light, deliberately light so she wouldn't wake him, but still she could feel the sleekness of his skin, the fluid power of his muscles, the pulsing warmth of his blood. She bent closer, her breath coming faster now, as she studied him.

She'd never looked so closely at another human being, had never been so curious before, but now she wanted to see everything of him. She studied the smooth bumps and hollows along his spine which reflected the bony vertebrae beneath. She looked at the shallow curves of his ribs, ran her fingers along the indentations between them, counting them. She was so close to him she could see every tiny hair of the fine down that covered him—her fingers so tautly sensitive now she could feel them lift against her skin when she drifted her hand against them.

How long she knelt, touching him like that, she had no idea, only that when her fingers slid beneath the sheet he stirred, and she froze, terrified.

She was still shaking when she reached the kitchen. For once the cats still slept, apparently oblivious to their mistress's distress, curled together in a small straw basket. Libby sank weakly onto a stool, watching them, waiting for her panicked breathing to slow. She was a pervert, she told herself numbly. A madwoman. He was unwell and in her care and she'd…assaulted him.

She shuddered, imagining what might have happened if he'd woken to find her bent over him like that. Would he have been furious? Disgusted?

William's head lifted and he looked directly at her and yawned. Leaving Duncan asleep, he climbed out of the basket, stretching each leg delicately as he strolled towards her and twined himself around her legs.

'You don't mind me touching you, do you?' she murmured, lifting the cat into her arms, enjoying his purr as he responded to her hands. She buried her face in his warm fur. 'You like it.'

There was a blur of movement by the door and then a voice. 'I liked it, too,' he said quietly.

Libby jumped. Slowly, very slowly, she lowered the cat. Dully she said, 'You were awake?'

He folded his arms and leaned against the doorframe, his broad chest bare, her duvet thickly rucked around his waist, his expression telling her the truth although he didn't speak.

She felt her face flood with colour. 'Why didn't you tell me?' she demanded. 'You should have stopped me.'

His eyes darkened and then there was a brief taut silence before he said, 'I need a shower.'

'Next to the bedroom.' She caught her lower lip between her teeth, concentrating on the simple practicalities. 'Soap in the basket. Spare towels and robes in the cupboard.'

She hadn't even asked about his headache, she reflected minutes later as she sat as if glued to the same seat, listening to the sound of the water flowing to the shower. 'Some nurse I am,' she told William forlornly. 'One look at him and everything sane flies straight out of my head.'

She heard the water being turned off and the sound galvanised her into action in a frantic race to delay the inevitable. She filled the kettle and put it on to boil, then laid out cups for tea. She opened cat food, smiling weakly as the sound propelled an immediately alert Duncan from bed to bowl. After dishing the cats their meal, she washed her hands and prepared breakfast.

By the time Alistair's friend reappeared, his chest now

covered by one of the robes she kept for her clients, there were two bowls of muesli waiting to be eaten and she was lifting the toast out of the toaster. 'How's the migraine?' she asked, keeping her voice bright in the hope that if she ignored what had happened he might do the same.

'There faintly still in the background.' He accepted the tea she passed him with a nod of acknowledgement. 'But usually I'm in pain for days,' he said, sitting on the stool she'd used earlier. He smiled at her. 'What was in the sandwich of yours? Pethidine?'

'Feverfew leaves.' One eyebrow rose and she felt herself flushing. 'It's a vasodilator,' she said quickly. 'That means it widens blood vessel—'

'I know what it means,' he said evenly.

'Oh.' Her hands shook as she passed him a plate and some toast. She gestured to the dishes of marmalade and jam she'd laid out. 'H-help yourself. You should eat.'

But he was watching her, not the food. 'Was your massage part of the treatment as well?'

She swallowed heavily. 'Massage helps drain tension and ease the cause of headaches.' She carried her plate across to the table, struggling to keep her expression calm as she took the chair opposite him. 'I was using oils. Lavender, marjoram, some camomile and ginger. The feverfew's a simple herbal remedy,' she added carefully. 'I didn't have any conventional drugs for your pain and you asked me not to call a doctor. I thought it might help.'

He took a mouthful of the tea she'd prepared then pulled a face. 'Revolting,' he declared. 'Another herb?'

'I didn't think you should drink coffee,' she said faintly. 'Caffeine does sometimes help in the beginning of a migraine but it can also be a trigger.'

'Libby, I'm sure you mean well but this is undrinkable.' But to her relief he looked amused, not angry, as he put the cup away from him and rubbed his eyes. 'Thank you for looking after me.'

She nodded. She'd loved looking after him but she didn't imagine he'd appreciate her telling him that. 'I didn't mind.'

Their eyes held for a few, disturbing seconds, but this time he broke the contact by reaching for her raspberry conserve. 'This looks home-made.'

'It's one of my grandmother's original recipes,' she said huskily.

His grin set her heart on fire. 'Of course it is,' he said softly. 'I shouldn't have needed to ask that.'

Their breakfast went well. He made no more references to her touching him but instead questioned her closely about burglary and crime rates locally. She reassured him that most of the crime that did occur was petty, involving car thefts and vandalism, and that she always kept a close eye on Alistair's cottage when he was away. But he seemed unconvinced because he asked her why she hadn't had an alarm system installed and if she'd ever thought about buying a dog.

Libby found it hard to understand why he should appear so concerned about what, for her, was such a minor issue, and she managed to steer the conversation away to the places he should be visiting during his stay in Cornwall.

'I'm here to work,' he told her wryly when she started to outline a tour which would take him to the major scenic sites around St Ives and Penzance. 'I don't have time for touring.'

She tilted her head, thirstily absorbing this first scrap of personal information about him. 'What sort of work?'

He pushed his empty plate away. 'Writing up two years' worth of research,' he explained. 'I was told to take my holidays and it seemed a good chance to get it done. I've been too busy to finish it until now.'

'Are you a journalist?' she asked. 'Is that how you know Alistair?'

He went very still. 'Libby, do you know who I am?'

'I know you're Alistair's friend—'

'My name?' he said dryly. 'Have I even introduced my-self?' His narrowed regard was abruptly amused now, and she realised that he hadn't, that she didn't even know his name, and that stunned her.

'I'm Nathan. Nathan Thomas.' He held out his hand to her and numbly she let it swallow hers. 'I'm Alistair's old-est brother.'

Nathan felt Libby's mental recoil from his announcement as tangibly as her small hand pulled sharply away from his. 'Alistair's brother?' she demanded huskily, as if she couldn't believe it. 'Nathan? *That* Nathan?'

'I never thought…' He lifted one shoulder, wondering what 'that Nathan' meant. 'It's absurd, but I forgot I hadn't told you.'

'You're the surgeon.'

'Yes.'

'I know about you.' When she lifted her hands and walked hesitantly to the opposite side of the room he saw her nails had left tiny semi-circular marks in the wooden table. 'You're the workaholic.'

'Possibly, according to Alistair,' he conceded slowly. His eyes narrowed on her as she bent to pick up one of her cats and hid her face in his fur while the cat glared at him with fierce yellow eyes. 'My career is demanding.'

She lifted her head, her face nervous and worried, and Nathan watched her speculatively, curious about what else Alistair could have said. But it seemed he wasn't about to find out, because she said faintly, 'I'm expecting someone. I'm sorry. Would you…?'

'I'm going,' he said flatly. Whatever Alistair had told her about him, it must have been bad. And, considering his thoughts about her over the last few days, it couldn't have been any worse than he deserved, he acknowledged wearily. Given not just his brother's prior claim but his own possible commitment to Paula. He pulled open her back door. 'Thanks again for last night.'

'Yes, fine.' Her voice was vague, distracted, and she wasn't even looking at him, her eyes instead on her cat. 'Fine.'

A glance at his watch when he reached Alistair's cottage told him that it was barely eleven but he needed a drink. Still in the towelling robe he'd put on after his shower, he went straight for the Scotch.

He tipped a generous triple into a tumbler then lifted the glass, but instead of downing it, as he'd intended, his fingers tightened and he hurled it into the fireplace, watching impassively as the impact of the glass smashing against the bricks sent tiny slivers of silver hurtling around the room.

Surprisingly, the gesture helped. Helped relieve some of his frustration at least, he reflected as he pulled on his jeans and trainers before sweeping up the mess. As well as reminding him of the appropriate response to his sudden urge for alcohol. He'd drowned more of the stuff in the four days he'd known Libby Deane than he'd drunk in the last two years. He didn't need any more.

He dumped the glass into the bin, wiped away the whisky, then switched on his computer, bringing up the files he'd started on the night before.

But half an hour later he shoved the machine aside, acknowledging wearily that the day was going to be another unproductive one. He prowled restlessly around the cottage. Picking up some of Alistair's photographs and souvenirs, he studied them silently. There were no photographs of Libby and he realised that Alistair had probably taken them with him to Brazil. But, unlike his brother, Nathan knew he didn't need photographs to remember how she looked. If he closed his eyes he could see her vividly.

And naked, he conceded dryly. Which wasn't good for his concentration.

The same way that remembering how she'd touched him wasn't good for it either. Expelling his breath slowly, he flung himself onto a rocking chair, his legs splaying to either side, and let his eyes close. No wonder he was finding it hard to work. He'd been awake before Libby had come into the room that morning. Awake but resting, his eyes closed while he'd tried to assess how bad his head was before he let the light in or tried to lift it.

Her first touch had been cool, assessing, clinical. But it had changed and he'd known he should have stopped her then but he'd been too weak.

The soft gasps of her breath, the rapid flutter of her pulse radiating from her wrists, the moist heat of her skin, the torturing brush of her hair along his spine when he'd felt her mouth close enough almost to taste him had told him that touching him was arousing her and that had almost driven him wild.

Only the repetition of Paula's and Alistair's names like a mantra in his head had stopped him from rolling aside and pulling her down onto him.

Nathan pushed himself out of the armchair, strode to the window and stared out at the grey slate roof of Libby's cottage. Today was Saturday. In one week Paula would be here with him and by then he'd know for sure if he was to be a father.

And if he wasn't to be? His mouth compressed. If he wasn't to be, it still couldn't make any difference. Even leaving aside his brother, and Libby's age, he had nothing to offer her. She belonged here and he didn't. He only hoped he remembered that the next time she came near him.

*   *   *

By Sunday afternoon Libby had worked herself into a state of near hysteria with worry. She'd been concerned the day before when the cottage had remained shut up all day, despite Nathan's car still being parked outside. She'd worried that his migraine might have come back, worried that he was alone and in pain and had, in fact, got as far as his back door before turning back, sick with nerves.

What if he was really ill? What if he'd…died?

She shuddered, pushing the horrifying thought aside although it had been haunting her for hours. Nobody died from a migraine, she told herself furiously. But what if his pain had been more than that? What if it had been a subarachnoid bleed? She'd once nursed a patient who'd survived a brain haemorrhage only to die from a second one two weeks later. He might be desperately ill.

Or he might be working, might want peace and quiet, she thought, struggling to keep some sense of normality about this. Perhaps, after yesterday, he was avoiding her. It wasn't hard to understand, given that her…massage must have embarrassed him. She covered her face with her hands, not wanting to think about it, but it came back anyway.

Alistair often talked about his family but it was Nathan who'd stuck in her mind. Nathan who had worried her. Nathan whom she'd thought about and been concerned about ever since, even though she'd never met him.

'He doesn't take holidays,' Alistair had said, 'so you'll probably never see him down here.' Alistair's voice had been light but Libby had known him well enough to guess at the unspoken emotion behind the words for there'd been more than a hint of hero-worship in the way he'd talked about his older brother.

'We're all worried he's going to work himself into an early grave,' he'd confided. 'His father died in his forties with a heart attack.' He'd already told her that Nathan and he had the same mother but different fathers. 'Nate is as fit as a horse and healthy but he needs to learn that there's more to life than work.'

Nathan's hard face floated before her vision and her hands clenched into fists. She couldn't bear the thought of anything happening to him.

Libby's hand was shaking when she lifted it to knock on his kitchen door. Expecting him to be half-dead, at the very least unconscious, she jumped back in fright when he jerked the door open.

His face was unshaven and irritated but there was nothing unhealthy about the impatience in his eyes. 'Yes?'

She took a hasty step back. 'I—I'm sorry,' she stammered, drinking in his strength, his vitality. 'I brought the painting you wanted.' She held it out.

He took it wordlessly, not even glancing at it, and she rushed on, 'Are you all right?'

'Of course.' He looked almost about to close the door on her but then he obviously saw her involuntarily flinch because his eyes softened. He sighed. 'I'm fine,' he said, more gently now. He rested the painting against the inside wall. 'The headache's gone. Libby, you don't have to worry about me.'

Her mouth felt parched and she swallowed heavily. 'I thought you might have been ill.'

'I've been trying to work.'

And now she was pestering him, she realised. 'I don't want to keep you,' she said abruptly. 'I hope you like the picture. Bye.'

'Wait!' He caught her as she turned away, his grip firm around her upper arm. He sighed. 'Sorry,' he said heavily. 'I guess I'm not in the best of moods. My work's not going as well as it should be but I didn't mean to take it out on you.'

She shook her head vaguely, his touch, his closeness, his heat, making her dizzy. 'It doesn't matter,' she said weakly.

'Yes, it does.' To her relief he released her arm but it was only so he could push the door wider. 'I need a break,' he told her, evenly now, his calmness making a mockery of her upheaval. 'Come in and I'll make you tea.'

Libby shook her head, not sure she was ready to cope with that. 'I was planning to go for a swim now.'

He frowned at her. 'The water's too rough today.'

'No, it's OK.' Not wanting his shrewd eyes to see too much because they might read her thoughts, she looked out towards the whitecaps beyond the bay entrance. 'It's not too rough for me. I'm much stronger than I look.'

'Libby, if you insist on going out in that, I'm coming with you.'

'Really, there's no need.' His words sent a jolt of panic spiralling through her chest. 'I've swum here since I was a child,' she said urgently. 'I can look after myself.'

He ignored her. 'Five minutes,' he ordered. 'I'll meet you at the steps.'

Back at her own cottage Libby fumbled her way into a swimsuit, her hands trembling so badly she could barely get the straps up. Duncan and William had uncurled themselves from their basket in the kitchen where they'd been taking their afternoon nap and stood in her bedroom doorway, watching her with identical puzzled frowns.

'A swim,' she told them, hauling her painting smock over her head to cover her costume. She pulled on her jeans, but left her feet bare. 'Just a swim. With Nathan.'

William promptly yawned and to Libby's surprise both cats strolled calmly back to their basket. She blinked at them. Normally the cats would have come with her to the beach and watched her swim. Perhaps they considered Nathan a safe companion?

Although 'safe' did not seem like an appropriate description for a man like Nathan, she reflected nervously, her legs shaky as she walked towards where he waited by the path. In fact, considering the way her pulse was fluttering, the word 'dangerous' seemed altogether more suitable.

His eyes dropped. 'What small feet you have,' he said softly. 'Like a child's.'

Libby's toes curled into the grass and his mouth quirked as he noted the embarrassed gesture, but to her relief he didn't comment. He nodded towards the path. 'You first.'

Too self-conscious to walk normally, she found herself scrambling awkwardly down the path and steps, but she didn't slip because although the track was narrow and steep she'd been up and down it so many times she could have done it blindfolded.

By the time she reached the beach the wind had whipped her hair free of its band and into a tangled mess around her face. While she stopped to re-tie it Nathan strode ahead.

Still wearing his jeans, he ran out to the water, bent to test it, then straightened, a grin lighting his face and taking her breath away. 'It's icy,' he complained.

His smile and the protest and the wind seemed to take hold of her tension and worries. Joy that he was all right and here on the beach with her suddenly welled up within her and she found herself laughing. 'It's good for you,' she shouted. 'Stop being so precious, you feeble Londoner.'

His grin broadened and he scooped up a handful of water. 'Come here and say that.'

She backed towards the cliff, still laughing, but her laughter trailed away as he stepped back onto dry sand and dropped his hands to the fastening of his jeans. He sent her a brief, almost mocking look, and she turned away, flustered.

Her movements slow and awkward, she stripped off her own jeans and her smock, and when she turned around he was already wading in, the water lapping the legs of his blue boxer-style swimmers.

Libby waited until he submerged before she ran down to the sea. She waded in until the cold water reached her knees then, catching her breath, she dived into a wave, surfacing a few yards from him.

He grinned. 'Race you.'

Libby was a good swimmer but her strength lay in stamina, not speed, and when Nathan stopped about fifty yards out from shore she was trailing him by a good dozen strokes. He didn't wait for her to catch up but instead flipped and swam directly for her, forcing her to stop and tread water to avoid hitting him. 'You're not fair,' she protested breathlessly. 'You're bigger than me. I should have had a head start.'

He flung his head back, his laugh at once triumphant and unrestrained, and Libby looked at him in wonderment, aching for him. 'I won fair and square,' he mocked, and then he looked at her and saw her watching him, and their eyes locked and everything changed.

The laughter drained out of his face, leaving only a fierce, hard determination that made her nerves tighten until she thought she might burst. Slowly he reached for her, grasped her shoulders then pulled her weakened body close to him so her breasts flattened against his chest. His head descended. 'And now,' he muttered thickly, 'I want my prize.'

CHAPTER SIX

NATHAN'S kiss was brief and hard and unsatisfying but it made Libby dizzy. She felt his hands slide to her buttocks, felt them cup her flesh, and then he was lifting her against him so her legs tangled with his and she couldn't tread water. She felt the sea lap her throat and then she was sinking. She grasped his shoulders. 'Nathan…'

'Open your mouth,' he muttered, the rawness of his voice making it a command, not a request.

Forgetting everything but him, she did and then he was kissing her again, touching her, and she couldn't believe it and she was melting and he was all water and salt, her desire and her universe, and it didn't matter that they were drowning.

Only he didn't let them. He forced her back, dragging her with fierce kicks to the light when she would have been content to drift downwards. She surfaced, coughing, tears streaming down her face, gasping for breath as Nathan kneaded her back. It took several minutes for her breathing to settle and even then her throat still rasped, burned by the salty water which had filled it moments before.

By the time she could see again, his face was wary, his jaw tense and controlled, no trace of the urgency or passion she'd imagined she'd seen before he'd kissed her. He pushed aside her hair which had fallen over her face, met her dazed eyes and seemed to flinch. 'Back to shore for you,' he said grimly.

He was still holding her, supporting her in the water, his hands under her arms, and she lifted her head in mute ap-

peal. Everything had been right with the world when he'd
been kissing her. 'Please…?'

'Please, what, Libby?' He looked angry, although
whether at himself or her she couldn't tell. 'Please, drown
you properly this time? Is that what you want?' His eyes,
darkened almost to black, flicked to the beach. 'I made a
mistake. I shouldn't have touched you.'

She felt her face flood with colour as reality rushed back.
He'd kissed her in fun, she realised, a simple gesture to
celebrate his victory. And she'd been deliriously happy,
happy enough to drown for something which had meant
nothing to him, had been only a momentary *mistake*. She
was a fool, pathetic. She was unbalanced. With the realisation came shame and anger at herself, and with her anger
the strength started to flow back into her limbs.

She kicked forward, forcing him to release her. Without
a word she swam for the beach, fast, faster than she'd ever
swum before, telling herself if she could just get there before him, get away from here, everything would be forgotten and life would go back to normal.

He caught her as she ran up the beach, and pulled her
back against him so hard the impact knocked her breath
away. 'It's not your fault,' he said harshly, as if he'd read
her thoughts. 'It's mine. You didn't do anything wrong.'

His grip on her arm gentled and she wrenched herself
away, scrambling away from him, but he caught her again.
'Stop it,' he muttered urgently, tugging her upright. 'Stop
running away.' He held her, stroking her arms the way he'd
done that afternoon up on the cliff. 'It's me who should be
ashamed, not you. I didn't think. We were under the water.
You were choking and I still didn't let you go. I could have
drowned you.'

'It was me letting *myself* drown,' she cried. 'I didn't
care.'

'That's not true. You were frightened.' He was wrong

but she had no breath to deny it. 'You should be angry with me.'

'I didn't care,' she repeated huskily, her throat so raw it hurt her to speak. Couldn't he understand? Hadn't he felt how she'd resisted him when he'd first tried to bring her up?

His hands tightened on her arms. 'I'm far stronger than you,' he insisted. 'I took advantage of that. You couldn't get away.'

'But I didn't want to get away,' she sobbed. 'All I wanted was for you never to stop.'

'No!' Strong arms slid round her, beneath her breasts, and he cradled her, rocking her gently from side to side. 'Hell!' he muttered. 'I'm sorry, Libby. I shouldn't have let myself near you.'

Desperately Libby tried to stop her tears, and with a huge effort of will she managed to stop her breath coming in the great heaves which were shaking her chest. She let herself lean back into his embrace, her eyes closing weakly. 'You saved my life,' she whispered.

'How can you say that?' he demanded against her forehead. 'I nearly killed you.'

That wasn't the point but she was too weak to argue, and now her tears had drained her of emotion. 'I didn't care,' she said faintly. All that mattered was that she stayed in his arms.

To her joy this time he didn't push her away. Instead, one hand shifted from her midriff to her hair. 'You're all tangled,' he said huskily.

She felt him tugging at her hairband and then her hair tumbled wet and heavy around her shoulders. Her eyes still closed, she felt him gather it together and gently wring out some of the surplus water, the drips sounding like soft rain on the sand beside them.

He slid his hand slowly through her hair, lifting the

strands, separating them, untangling them. As his hand moved his knuckles grazed her shoulders, her back, her hips, her buttocks, brushing her so lightly she knew he could be barely aware of it, but he heated her, made her ache.

Over and over again he brushed her, slowly, over and over until felt herself arching like one of her cats, numbed by the sheer sensual pleasure of his touch.

His hand paused and she made a soft noise of protest, but he was only turning her to face him, bending her head so her forehead rested against his chest. Keeping her head bent, he began stroking her neck and the sensitive skin behind her ears.

Her eyes still shut, she could hear the steady beat of his heart and the sound was wonderful. He smoothed the drying hair down her back, using both hands, gently caressing her spine. She heard his heart rate increase.

'Libby…?' he said hoarsely, his voice rumbling through his chest against her ear. 'Libby, that's enough.'

She lifted her head, blinking, dazed by the light and by him, and he tilted her chin up and forced her to meet his dark, glittering gaze.

'Go home,' he ordered roughly. 'Fetch your clothes and go up to the cottage.'

She looked longingly at his mouth, wishing she had the courage to kiss him.

'Home, Libby.' His mouth tightened as if he'd guessed her thoughts, and he put her firmly away from him. 'Please. Now.'

Her legs were so weak that she swayed, but he didn't touch her and, trembling, abandoned, she turned away, walking forlornly towards where she'd left her things at the bottom of the path. Slowly she made her way up towards the cottage.

She turned around once, near the top, but he wasn't following her, wasn't even looking at her. Instead, he was running towards the water and while she watched he dived in, easy, fluid strokes taking him quickly back out into the bay.

By Tuesday afternoon Nathan had had enough of his self-imposed imprisonment in Alistair's cottage. He pushed aside his laptop and moved restlessly around the room. Working much of Sunday night and all day Monday, it meant he'd made reasonable headway on his work, but the sun looked warm and the sky was clear and suddenly he longed to be anywhere but locked up in the cottage with his computer.

And he could handle Libby. He'd lost control once, yes, *temporarily*, but it wouldn't happen again. He was a man, not an animal, he reminded himself. A man with a con-science and morals and, he'd thought, integrity and a sense of loyalty.

He grimaced. Not such noble thoughts, he conceded heavily. His so-called conscience and morals hadn't helped him when he'd really needed them. The only thing that had stopped him had been the appalling realisation that he'd almost drowned her.

For the umpteenth time he studied the water-colour she'd given him, finding pleasure in the gentle, sun-washed scene. He still owed her money for this although she hadn't said how much. She might need it, he told himself. She probably didn't have a lot of money. It wasn't fair to delay giving her what he owed her.

Her back door was open but instead of Libby two other women were sitting in her kitchen. He hesitated but the woman sitting nearest the door, a ruddy-cheeked, red-haired woman, looked up and beamed. 'Hello,' she said cheer-fully, standing to greet him, her accent pure rolling Cornwall. 'You're Alistair's friend.'

'Brother,' Nathan corrected automatically.

Two sets of eyebrows lifted speculatively and he had the uncomfortable experience of being thoroughly assessed by both women. Apparently he was judged satisfactory because the second woman, a frail, elderly woman with grey-white hair, stood as well. 'Libby won't be long,' she announced waveringly. 'Tea?'

'Er…' Nathan hesitated, but it appeared they weren't going to take no for an answer because a third cup had already been produced and some dark, fearful-looking brew was being poured for him. He walked inside and when they sat again he took a seat. 'Thank you.' He looked down into the cup but refrained from taking any.

'She's with a client,' the younger woman explained, leaving Nathan, who'd assumed Libby earned her income from her art, none the wiser.

She tapped the side of her nose knowingly. 'Boyfriend trouble.'

He started. 'Libby?'

They both laughed then exchanged irritatingly knowing looks. 'Megan,' the same woman said smugly. She tilted her chin, regarding him with steely blue eyes. 'Libby doesn't have a boyfriend.'

Wondering why they didn't know about Alistair, he took a mouthful of the tea they'd prepared, catching his breath at the brew's awful, grassy sweetness.

'She's giving Megan a potion.' The grey-haired woman was watching him closely. 'Libby has the gift.'

Sensing from her expression that some reply was expected, he echoed, 'The gift?'

'Mmm,' the younger woman confirmed. 'That's right.'

He took another sip of the ghastly tea. 'How…useful,' he said finally.

They both beamed at him. 'She's fixed my leg,' the

frailer of the two said, lifting her skirt so he could see one bandaged shin.

To his alarm she promptly began to unwind the crêpe. 'There's no need,' he said hastily. 'I believe you. I'm sure it's best left clean and covered.'

'You should see.' The younger woman leaned over to help her companion. 'It's a miracle.' She stripped away the bandage then lifted away a strip of non-adhesive dressing, to reveal what seemed to have been a large pre-tibial laceration, surprisingly, considering the woman's age and the fragility of her skin, almost healed.

Nathan noted the clean granulating tissue with relief—he'd been half expecting some gaping, horrendously infected ulcer. It seemed that sort of conversation. 'Very healthy,' he said evenly. 'Shouldn't be long before that closes.'

'Over a year I had that,' he was told. 'Getting worse and worse. Doctor told me it would never heal. He said I needed plastic surgery and skin grafts but he didn't want to send me for it because we were both sure the operation would kill me.'

Nathan sighed. 'Really?'

She nodded keenly. 'District Nurse every day for months I had. Antibiotics?' She lifted her arms expansively. 'Antibiotics until they were coming out my ears.' She tilted her chin. 'Marigold leaves,' she said firmly.

Once again he realised he was expected to say something but his mind was blank and after a few seconds she continued. 'Also comfrey under the bandage for a few weeks,' she confided, 'but it was the marigold leaves that did the trick.'

'Five weeks,' the younger woman added. 'Five weeks from a great, gangrenous hole in her leg to this.'

Nathan winced. 'I'm impressed.' He took his third sip of tea and it wasn't tasting any better.

'And my…problems,' the younger woman said obliquely. 'I've been uncomfortable and sore for five years. A month of Libby's treatment and two massages a week to relax me and I'm enjoying myself with the husband again.' Her bold gaze didn't falter and it was Nathan who finally looked away. 'If you know what I mean,' she added pointedly.

He thought he might but he wasn't about to try and clarify the point. Briefly he debated making some excuse and leaving, but before he could move he heard Libby's softly husky voice in the hall. A few seconds later she walked into the kitchen, her eyes widening with obvious shock as they locked with his.

'Oh,' she said faintly. 'You're here.'

He stood. 'I'll come back later,' he said quickly, drinking in her sweet beauty, irritated with himself but unable to stop his gaze skimming the slender lines of her body beneath the businesslike white uniform she was wearing. But he wasn't blind to her discomfort, her flush and the sudden panicky lifting of her chest as easy to read as neon signs. 'You're busy.'

But the red-haired woman took control. 'Libby, you see Isabel now,' she said firmly. 'Her husband's waiting in the car. And I'll keep…?' Arched eyebrows turned to him.

'Nathan,' Nathan said wearily.

She beamed. 'Nathan,' she repeated. 'I'm Monica.' She looked back to Libby. 'I'll keep Nathan company. Till you're free. I'm sure we'll find loads to talk about.'

Nathan registered Libby's obvious discomfort at the arrangement, but Monica's determination was clear and a few minutes later he found himself sitting alone with the other woman.

'So, Nathan.' She smiled carefully, almost, he thought faintly, like a snake about to strike. 'Are you married or divorced?'

'Single,' he said warily. 'Do you live locally, Monica?'

'Not far.' She leaned forward a little, bracing her arms on the table. 'How long will you be with us?'

'Until Alistair returns from South America.'

'Why, that's wonderful.' He was graced with another beam. 'Cornwall's so beautiful at this time of year.' She tilted her head. 'You don't look like Alistair.'

'Different fathers,' he found himself revealing. 'Alistair looks very much like my stepfather.'

'Ah-h.' Her regard softened. 'Your father is…?'

'He died when I was a child.'

She poured herself another cup of tea, offering him the pot which he firmly turned down. Then she said, 'Libby lost both parents when she was very young.'

'She mentioned she'd been brought up by her grandmother.'

'Car accident,' Monica told him. 'Driving down from London. Libby was just a toddler. She was thrown clear. She was brought up by her grandmother, you're right. Elspeth was an expert on herbs and potions.' Her sharp eyes held his. 'Some round here called her a witch but that didn't stop them coming to her if they were ill or in need.'

Inwardly he smiled, wondering if that was what they'd meant earlier about Libby having 'the gift'.

As if sensing his scepticism, Monica's face tightened. 'She's a fully trained nurse,' she said flatly. 'A real nurse, I mean. Staff nurse, I think they're called these days. She's got all the certificates. Did you know that?'

'No, I didn't.' He was surprised. In his experience nurses were invariably practical, earthy people. Libby seemed too ethereal.

'She trained up in London,' Monica was saying. 'She stayed a little while, working, but after Elspeth died she came home for good. This is where she belongs.' She paused significantly, her gaze uncomfortably direct. 'She's content here but she's not an old woman like her grand-mother. It's not good for her to be alone. She needs more than two cats for company.'

'There's Alistair,' Nathan said abruptly.

Monica sniffed. 'Alistair is Alistair,' she told him cryptically. 'Even if he is your brother.'

One of Libby's big black cats propelled itself up onto his knees, saving him from having to come up with any answer to that puzzling observation. Absently he stroked the creature under the chin, to be rewarded by a low purring sound as the animal nuzzled his hand and after one or two gentle stomps curled himself up into a neat coil.

'William likes you,' said Monica smugly. 'That's a good sign if there's to be any future for you here. He's normally the wary one.'

'I live in London,' Nathan remarked evenly, keeping his expression deliberately bland. He agreed with her statement that Libby belonged where she was but that didn't change anything in his life. 'London's where I work and it's where I belong. I like my life there. I have no intention of moving.'

He thought he'd made his point strongly enough but Monica didn't appear abashed. 'People give up all sorts of things for love,' she said smoothly.

He looked down at William, scratching the appreciative cat around his ears, debating how best to extract himself from the conversation without offending Libby's friend. Thankfully he didn't have to because at that moment he heard voices in the hall and then Libby was back. She looked almost surprised to see him still there but once again Monica took control.

'He's happy enough,' she told Libby, glancing in Nathan's direction as if he were some sort of recalcitrant infant. 'He'll wait.'

He saw Libby's throat make a convulsive movement.

'Very well,' she said huskily. She ushered Monica through into the hall then looked back at Nathan, her brow creased. 'This might take some time,' she said quickly. 'You really shouldn't wait.'

Nathan looked down just as William looked up at him, the yellow cat eyes demanding he stay. 'I'm fine,' he told Libby. 'Comfortable. No hurry.'

But it didn't seem long before he heard their voices again in the corridor. Monica poked her head around the door and winked at him before she left.

Libby appeared shortly after. She'd changed into faded jeans and a colourful T-shirt and had let her hair loose, and his eyes narrowed with appreciation. He only tore his gaze away from her when she came across towards him and William dug irritated claws into his thigh.

'I came to ask about the painting,' he said neutrally, resuming his petting of the animal so the cat would relax again. 'You didn't tell me how much I owed you.'

Her eyelids fluttered down, concealing her eyes, but not before he'd recognised her nervousness. 'Consider it a gift,' she said, 'for saving my life.'

Nathan tensed. 'We've already discussed that,' he pointed out. 'You don't owe me anything.'

She moved gracefully around to the other side of the table and scooped up the kettle. 'Then ten pounds.' She emptied the remains of the tea into a large plastic bucket by the bench.

'You're humouring me,' he chided dryly. 'We both know I'd pay a lot more than that in a shop.'

'Not much more than twenty.' She still didn't turn around to him. 'More tea?'

He was amazed to hear himself suddenly laughing, and her wide-eyed astonishment as she turned around increased his amusement. 'Libby,' he managed, 'that tea is the vilest thing I've ever tasted. Worse even than the last batch you foisted on me. I almost retched. If you really want to drive me away you only have to ask me to leave.'

'But I don't.' For a few seconds her pale brow was creased into a concerned frown but suddenly she relaxed into a gentle smile which made his pulse thud. 'I'm sorry,' she said huskily. 'It wasn't tea they gave you. It was Mrs Spalding's infusion.'

'Marigold leaves?'

She looked puzzled. 'Among other things,' she admitted. 'It probably doesn't taste very pleasant.'

He wasn't going to argue with that. 'How about coffee?'

She hesitated, the frown back again making her look like a worried child. 'I don't keep any here. I've plenty of vodka, or else there's some brandy somewhere.'

Nathan grimaced. The last thing he needed was more alcohol. 'Never mind.' He watched her make tea, acutely aware of her self-consciousness but knowing there was nothing he could say to relieve it. What had happened on the beach on Sunday had happened. The best thing for both of them was never to mention it again.

When her drink was made she took the seat opposite him, finally looking at him again. 'I'm sorry about William,' she said, her eyes dropping to her cat. 'Once he's settled he's hard to budge.'

'He's all right.' He continued to tickle beneath the animal's ears. 'I didn't know you were a nurse.'

'Monica's been talking.'

'She only mentioned it in passing. Where did you train?'

'In London.' She took some of her tea. 'The York.'

He nodded. The York was one of the oldest London teaching hospitals, although in recent years it had suffered more cuts in funding than most and many wards and the once superb casualty department had been forced to close. 'So, what are you doing now?' he asked. 'District nursing?'

She stared down into her drink, her shoulders lifting as

if she was taking a deep breath. 'My interest is in alternative therapies,' she said quietly. 'Natural remedies and massage. I use some of my nursing experience but I don't consider myself a nurse in the conventional sense of the word
any longer.'

'Your two patients this morning are obviously impressed.'

Her eyes flew to his face. 'I thought you'd be scathing.'

'Why?'

'You're a surgeon.'

'I suppose that means I do need convincing,' he admitted. He disengaged William's claws where the cat had dug
into his leg again and stroked the cat to soothe him again.
'I'm not an enthusiast of alternative medicine. In my work
I deal in black and white. Plumbing, if you like. I admit
I'm biased towards orthodox medicine and I've seen problems when orthodox treatment's been delayed. But that
doesn't mean my mind is closed. Unless you're talking
about quacks who diagnose fake diseases which they then
charge a fortune to cure.' His mouth tightened. 'I consider
them con artists pure and simple.'

She nodded slowly. 'Of course I agree with that.'

'As a nurse,' he added, 'I'm sure you're careful about
what you do. Clearly you've helped the woman with the
pre-tibial laceration and something certainly cleared up my
migraine faster than any other one I've had.'

She smiled ruefully. 'Nathan, you don't really believe it
was my treatment.'

He smiled. She'd seen through him. 'OK I'm still a
cynic,' he admitted. 'Personally I doubt those leaves and
the massage did anything. I think careful care and time
cured the laceration and whatever...' his mouth twitched
'...problems were ailing Monica, but I'm prepared to leave
it open. All right?'

She smiled again, a soft, gentle smile this time which warmed his heart. 'All right,' she agreed.

He wanted more smiles. 'Why don't you tell me about the sorts of things you treat?' he said carefully. 'Teach me something.'

Those beautiful green eyes widened so far he thought he might just about drown in them. 'Are you serious?'

'Of course. I'm...sceptical but interested.'

Libby's mouth formed a surprised 'O' but she seemed to believe him. 'What do you want to know?'

Everything about you, he thought, but he couldn't ever tell her that and so his reply was conventional. 'What do you treat? How do you know what to use? Those sorts of things.'

She lifted one slim shoulder. 'I treat most simple things—stress, allergies, skin problems, digestive problems,' she explained. 'A couple of local GPs have been sending clients to me, and if I'm worried that something's not as simple as it appears, or I need a medical opinion, I either send people to a medical herbalist or back to their doctors.' She took a few sips of her tea. 'Learning what to use isn't difficult. I've studied extensively and my grandmother taught me a great deal. After so long it becomes almost...instinctive.'

'Really?'

He'd meant the word as polite encouragement but from the sudden flare of anger in her face he knew she'd misinterpreted him. 'Over fifty per cent of modern drugs derive from plants and moulds or are chemical copies of plant products,' she said fiercely. 'Aspirin, digoxin, penicillin, quinine and hundreds of others were all used by herbalists for centuries before physicians "discovered" them.' Her eyes glowed vivid, startling emerald. 'Ancient Egyptians laid mouldy bread on infected wounds thousands of years before penicillin was isolated from the same mould.'

He lifted his hands defensively. 'I believe you,' he said, entranced by her vibrancy. 'I'm not arguing.'

'Oh.' Her face coloured faintly and she seemed to falter. 'I'm sorry,' she murmured, her eyes lowering to the table. 'That's my nursing experience again. Doctors can be quite scathing when people discuss alternative therapies. I thought you were mocking me.'

Curious, for he'd never considered anything but medicine he asked, 'You never wanted to be a doctor yourself?'

She looked up sharply, as if looking for criticism in that remark too but whatever she saw in his face must have reassured her because her reply was quite calm. 'Never.'

'Why?'

She seemed to bristle. 'Even if I'd had the marks to gain admission, it wouldn't have been right for me,' she told him quickly. 'I don't accept many of the precepts of orthodox medicine. I don't think using toxic drugs to treat symptoms rather than the whole person is the right approach.'

'Yet you nursed.'

'I thought nursing was about caring for patients.'

'Isn't it?'

'It doesn't seem to be these days.' She was flustered now. He could see it in the restlessness of her hands, the way she flicked her hair back, but she didn't refuse to answer. 'I found the reality of nursing was awful. Resources were so stretched at the York that even as a final-year student and first-year graduate I was left in charge of whole wards. Sometimes I was the only registered nurse on duty. I felt as if I had no time to spend with my patients. I couldn't really talk with them or care for them. I had too many people to look after and too many forms to fill in, computer entries to make, students to supervise, budgets to propose.'

Her face tensed as all her doubts came tumbling out. 'I wasn't really helping anyone,' she said finally. 'Aside from my knowledge of herbal medicine, during my training I studied aromatherapy and massage, thinking that I could use that, particularly with my elderly patients, in hospitals. I didn't once have time to spare to use those skills. Not once.' She sighed.

'All I was doing was trying to get from day to day, propping up a system which was putting money ahead of patients, regardless of what was the best type of care. It wasn't what I wanted of my life.'

He felt a pang of recognition as she echoed many of his own doubts about his work. The difference was she'd had an alternative. 'So you left.'

'It wasn't that easy,' she admitted hesitantly. 'My grandmother's death was the catalyst. After that I realised…' She stopped and gave him a small, embarrassed smile. 'I'm sorry,' she said faintly. 'You can't really be interested in this.'

But Nathan frowned. 'Go on.'

She hesitated fractionally, her expression doubtful, but at his urging she continued slowly, 'My grandmother had a very simple life here—enjoying her garden, studying her remedies and looking after her cats—but she was very happy and she genuinely helped the people she treated. After she died I realised that that was the sort of life I wanted for myself.' Her lashes came down and concealed her eyes from him. 'And now I have it.'

Her words reinforced his own certainty about how completely she belonged to this cottage and this bay, and he envied her her contentment. But didn't she miss the excitement of city life? 'No regrets?'

She shook her head. 'None,' she said simply. 'I love it here. I can spend an hour, two hours with someone if I need to. And what I do helps without harm.'

He tilted his head. 'Does it pay the bills?'

'I don't charge.' The tilt of her small chin was almost defiant as she met his surprised expression. 'People bring me things,' she explained. 'Food from their gardens, fruit, baking, meat for the cats. Some do bring me money, and that's all right if it's what they prefer, but I don't need it. My parents were reasonably...well off. When I reached eighteen I came into quite a lot of money...' She stopped, her brow creasing. 'I like to think they would have approved,' she said distantly.

'They couldn't not approve,' Nathan said quietly, watching her, sensing her distraction. If he'd been more certain of his control he'd have touched her hand reassuringly, but that was a risk he still wasn't confident he could take. 'Tell me about your herbs, Libby. Do you grow them yourself?'

Her lovely face cleared. 'Quite a few,' she said. 'Shall I show you my garden?'

'Why not?' he said heartily, his reward her shy smile. He dislodged the protesting William from his knees and walked to the front door, waiting for Libby to precede him.

As she passed he caught the drifting scent that rose from her throat. It was the soft, floral scent that to him was Libby, and it captivated him, captivated him like the almost imperceptible movement of her small breasts beneath her T-shirt, like the firm jut of her buttocks and the fluid length of her thighs beneath the worn cloth of her jeans.

For a few seconds while she moved gracefully across the grass towards her garden he stayed by the door, his expression frozen, his body tightening with the ache to touch those breasts.

Paula and Alistair, he recited mentally. Paula and Alistair. 'Nathan, you need them tattooed on your hands,' he muttered, only half in jest, before he followed Libby outside.

CHAPTER SEVEN

FRIDAY evening Libby hummed as she prepared for dinner. The meal was going to be simple, pasta and salad, her work that day had gone well and, most of all, she thought, hugging the knowledge to herself like a special prize, Nathan would be joining her for the meal.

She twisted her hair into a knot on top of her head, pinned it, then scooped up Duncan and looked earnestly into his creased little face. 'Nathan's not remotely like all those horrible narrow-minded doctors I used to work with,' she told him.

The last three days had shown her that much and more. When he'd suggested on Tuesday that she teach him some of her methods she'd at first suspected he was only being kind by humouring her. But she'd been wrong.

He'd proved himself a keen learner and had even put aside his own work to spend the last three afternoons with her. While she sensed he remained at best sceptical, he had been telling the truth about his open mind. He was interested and enthusiastic. He listened to her and was never patronising. And she loved him so madly she tingled.

'*Desperately*,' she told Duncan. 'Absolutely desperately.'

If the hours with him had been almost torture, it had been a sweet, tender torture which had electrified her. She felt as if she'd never been properly alive before. She lowered Duncan and stretched, enjoying the sensuous slide of her muscles as they tautened. Her skin felt newly awakened. Even the gentle rub of her clothes seemed charged with illicit, dangerous pleasure.

She lowered her arms with a soft sigh. It was painfully obvious her feelings weren't returned. She knew he must sense some of her emotions for there was a tenseness about him sometimes and the care he took to avoid touching her, even by accident, was extreme. Still, the way he'd kissed her that day in the sea had given her hope, and she clung to the memory of it like algae to a rock.

'He likes me a little,' she told the attentive Duncan firmly as she stepped into the dress she'd bought in Truro on an impulsive shopping trip the evening before. 'And that's a start.'

Nathan tapped on the window then walked straight in through the open door just as she was checking on the lasagne in the Aga. Libby straightened awkwardly, his shrewdly assessing gaze turning her even more self-conscious than usual. 'Oh,' she said faintly. 'You're early.'

'A few minutes.' His voice was very low. He made a vague gesture towards his casual jeans and open-necked blue shirt. 'I didn't realise we were dressing up. Shall I change?'

'Of course not.' Nervously she ran a smoothing hand across the amber linen of her sleeveless dress, then saw his eyes narrow speculatively on the movement and she flushed. 'You look nice.' Even in his casual clothes he was darkly disturbing, too knowing for her peace of mind, she acknowledged. 'I just felt like wearing something other than jeans or shorts for a change.'

One shoulder lifted doubtfully but he didn't comment and instead merely held up the bottle of red wine he'd brought. 'OK?'

'Fine.' She turned back to the oven, busying herself with controls which didn't need any attention while she tried to regain her composure. 'There's an opener thing in the top drawer.' She waited until she heard the pop of the wine being uncorked before turning around. 'It's only lasagne,' she said rather shrilly. 'I hope you like it.'

'Relax, Libby.' His eyes dropped to her hands where they twisted anxiously at her sides, belying the deliberate lightness of her tone. 'After days of tinned soup and sandwiches, lasagne sounds terrific.'

She put her hands behind her back and frowned. 'You should have told me,' she said, the words coming out in a rush. 'I could have prepared meals for you—'

'Stop.' He looked amused but his voice was low and firm, tolerating no argument. 'No. I didn't mean it like that. I haven't needed your help.'

And hadn't wanted it either, she registered, reading between the lines.

He indicated the wine. 'Shall I pour you some?'

She rarely drank alcohol but, not wanting to appear any more unsophisticated that she must already seem, Libby accepted the glass he passed her. She took a wary sip and murmured something vaguely appreciative, although the taste reminded her of little other than cranberries turned musty from long storage.

Carefully she put the glass aside, ignoring the lazy amusement in his eyes as he noted the gesture. He himself took a long swallow, then another, apparently enjoying the flavour. 'It's good for you,' he said easily. 'Reduces the risk of heart disease and lowers cholesterol.'

'Try garlic, oats and ginseng,' she murmured. 'None of which addle your brain.'

He laughed. 'Sometimes pleasure's worth the risk,' he told her mockingly. 'Are you a teetotaller?'

'Not at all,' she said stiffly, feeling foolish. She took a hurried second sip of the wine, then several more, startled by the way the insides of her mouth puckered in protest. 'Anything in moderation.'

'Hmm?' He tilted his head, his eyes teasing. 'Anything?'

She felt a blush of colour sweep up from the high neck of her dress but forced herself to meet his gaze. 'Almost anything,' she said carefully, not sure where this could be leading. 'Within reason.'

'Within reason?' His voice was very deep. 'What if your…' he paused, his gaze dark and probing, infinitely disturbing '…desires are beyond reason?'

Libby faltered. Recognising that she was hopelessly out of her depth with him like this, her eyes flickered nervously away. She heard him mutter something roughly under his breath but when he spoke again his voice was absolutely neutral.

'The lasagne smells delicious.'

Clutching at the excuse his remark provided, she turned back to the range, bending to check on the dish. It was cooked, the pasta softened and fragrant with tomatoes and aubergine and oregano, the cheesy top bubbling and browned, and she lifted it out. While she waited for it to settle she bustled around, avoiding his eyes as she grated extra Parmesan then prepared a salad.

To her relief Nathan changed the conversation completely. 'That feverfew you fed me for my migraine,' he said. 'I'm interested in knowing more about it. If it really does work as a vasodilator it's potentially useful for some vascular patients, and vascular surgery's my speciality. Is it already used in a drug?'

'I've heard rumours about an extract being made available on prescription.' She frowned. 'I'm surprised you don't already know about it. The *Lancet* ran a series of articles on it years ago. I assumed that meant it had become almost orthodox.'

'If it has I'm not up with it.' He tilted his head. 'At least not with the herb itself, although I may know the drugs if there're some derived from it. What's the mechanism of action supposed to be?'

'My books suggest it's the vasodilator effect,' she told him. 'Also, there's some thought that it inhibits the release of migraine-triggering agents from white cells and platelets.' She smiled. 'How's that? Scientific enough for you?'

He returned her smile. 'I'm not sure I like it,' he said softly. 'You're destroying your own mystique.'

His gentle regard was oddly unsettling and she hastily looked away again. As if sensing her embarrassment, his next question was crisply businesslike. 'Do you know what the active ingredient is?'

'There will be several. I don't remember any specific names but I could look them up,' she said, keeping her head lowered, pretending to concentrate on the red pepper she was slicing for the salad. 'But, Nathan, whole parts of the plant are important. Different elements balance each other. Extract one ingredient and you lose that harmony.'

She glanced up to see him grinning at her. 'Of course,' he said lightly. 'How could I have forgotten yesterday's lesson?'

She relaxed at that, and they slid gently back into the pattern of the last few days. 'The plant's also an anti-inflammatory,' she told him, 'an anti-prostaglandin, so it's useful for acute arthritis and period pains related to pelvic congestion, and an infusion makes a good uterine stimulant post-delivery.'

His brows lifted. 'Impressive.'

'Although there are side effects,' she admitted. 'Mouth ulcers.'

'Ah!' He tilted his head. 'Hence your question about that when I was ill.'

'That's right.' Libby scooped the rest of the vegetables into a large wooden bowl. 'I only had the leaves in stock, not the tincture, so if you did suffer from ulcers I would have tried something completely different.'

'Such as?'

She deposited the salad bowl on the table. 'Lavender or rosemary, for instance. Perhaps peppermint.' Using oven mitts, she carried the lasagne across and sliced him a generous portion. 'Sometimes the simple things are best. Actually, there are quite a few options for migraine but I've found that if feverfew's suitable for the client then it's the best—although its strength is really more in prevention rather than treatment itself. You were lucky.'

He smiled. 'Or it was never going to be a severe migraine.'

So she hadn't erased his doubts. Chiding herself for wanting to convince him, she said quietly, 'Of course.'

After the meal he helped her wash up. As he dried her plates he asked, 'How long have you been vegetarian?'

She looked up from scrubbing the lasagne dish, startled, realising she hadn't thought to warn him. 'For ever.' She frowned. 'I'm sorry. I suppose you were expecting meat.'

He lifted one shoulder, as if it hadn't bothered him unduly but Libby felt awful. Meat-eaters were used to a lot of protein. He was probably still starving. 'I've some steak in the fridge,' she said quickly. 'Monica gives it to me for the cats but it's always very good quality.'

He laughed. 'Relax. I've eaten plenty.' William and Duncan were rolling playfully together on the floor, batting at each other like two miniature bears, and he sent them a quick sideways glance. 'Besides, even if I was starving I wouldn't touch it. The monsters might not appreciate their food disappearing.'

She smiled, handing him the clean dish to dry. 'You're exaggerating,' she chided. 'They like you.'

His mouth compressed and suddenly the atmosphere thickened. 'They don't know me,' he said smoothly.

Libby felt herself tense. They knew him as well as she did and she loved him. 'They *do* like you,' she insisted stiffly. 'Very much.'

He went very still. 'They don't know me,' he repeated, emphasising each separate word. 'Any more than you do.'

Avoiding his eyes, Libby lifted the plug to drain the sink, then wiped the bench and removed her washing gloves. Nervously she said, 'You're kind to them. You pet them and play with their ball. That's how cats judge people.'

Out of the corner of her eye she caught the blur of movement as he tossed his teatowel back towards its rack. Then he was beside her, his hip abutting the bench, his arms folded, his expression brooding. 'Libby, don't make the mistake of judging me by the same criteria your cats have chosen.'

She swallowed, clutching her hands together nervously. 'You've never been unkind to me.'

He muttered something harsh and pointed beneath his breath, his mouth twisting as he registered her involuntary recoil. 'You're unbelievably naïve,' he said softly.

She tilted her head, resenting that. 'I'm not a child.'

His eyes darkened as they slid assessingly down her figure, leaving disturbing little trails of sensation across her skin. 'So I see.' His gaze lingered on her mouth, so long she felt it swell. 'In that dress and with your hair up you almost look your age.'

She flushed, lifting a shaky hand to smooth the coil on the top of her head, not understanding why she was suddenly wishing she'd stayed in her jeans. She'd wanted to look older and more worldly, hadn't she? That had been the whole idea. 'Good.'

His eyes lifted to her hair. 'Take it down.'

She froze, a sudden pulse of heated blood flooding her lower abdomen. He'd never spoken to her like that before, never, and his low command turned the air between them suddenly warm and heavy. 'W-what?'

He didn't move. 'Your hair, Libby. Take it down.'

Responding involuntarily to his demand, her hands

reached for the clasp, but instead of undoing it she looked up at him, bewildered but needing to understand. 'Why?'

'To remind me that you're not as grown-up as you look tonight,' he said grimly. Obviously impatient with her inept fumbling he reached for her, brushing her shaky hands aside. His fingers tugged once, twice, and then, released from its constraints her hair tumbled down, free and heavy.

Libby caught her breath at the silky slide of it against the skin the low-cut back of the dress had left bare, and as if Nathan were attuned to her every emotion his eyes narrowed assessingly.

'What a little sensualist you are,' he said softly. 'How the hell does Alistair keep his hands to himself?'

'Alistair and I are friends,' she said thickly, finding it hard to breathe while he was watching her so intently. 'That's all.'

His mouth tightened as if her reply irritated him. 'He'll be home in two weeks and everything will be normal again.'

'Because you'll be back in London again,' she said weakly, adding the words he hadn't. 'But you're still here now. Do you want to kiss me, Nathan?'

'No.' But he lifted his hand and grazed her lower lip with the pad of his thumb, rubbing gently until her mouth parted and his nail scraped her teeth. 'Tell me to leave,' he ordered huskily.

She couldn't. 'You don't know what you're asking,' he added roughly, backing her until the edge of the stone bench jutted hard against her lower back.

She did know what she was asking. She knew exactly, and with a sound that was halfway between anger and frustration his hands slid beneath her, gathered up her dress and hoisted her up so she sat on the bench, her head level with his. 'Libby,' he murmured, still holding himself away from her, 'you're a very beautiful girl and you're very desirable but I'm not going to touch you. I can't.'

Holding her breath, half-crazed by her own daring, she guided his hand to her breast. For a moment he resisted but then, gloriously, instead of rejecting her, it closed slowly around her soft fullness. 'You see, you can,' she said faintly, tipping her head back, the words seeming to come from someone else, someone…confident and womanly. She let her eyes close, concentrating on her body's response, intoxicated by the exquisite sweetness of his touch.

The way she was sitting on her dress had pulled the cloth taut over her nipple, and when he nudged it, scratched it through the tense fabric, tiny strings of sensation tugged deep within her and she gasped. She pulled at his head, trying to force him closer, not understanding what she needed but knowing only he could give it to her.

Although his head lowered, his body didn't move and still he didn't kiss her. Instead, his mouth moved, lingered beside her throat, then her cheeks, her ears, teasing her as his hands stroked her breasts until she burned and murmured for more. But still he wouldn't kiss her, his mouth staying close to her skin, gliding so near her she could feel the warmth of his breath, but never touching her.

Her breath was coming in short panting gasps. She lifted herself higher, trying to reach his mouth, but all he let her kiss was his chin and she ached with frustration, needing the touch of his mouth the way he'd touched her that day in the sea but too shy to ask again.

Still holding himself away from her, his hands dropped to grip her thighs. Too weak to hold herself up, she rested her palms on the bench behind her, her body arching towards him. His eyes locked with hers, as if asking permission, but she'd have denied him nothing, watching breathlessly as he carefully rolled up the rest of her dress until her knees were clear. Then his eyes dropped and slowly, very slowly, he parted her legs.

When he lifted his eyes again, seconds or perhaps minutes later, his skin was flushed dark but his face was closed to her. They were both breathing quickly but Libby could see his control and it scared her. Suddenly cold, she straightened, looking down at the way his fingers still dug softly into the taut flesh of her thighs and wondering how she could be cold when he was touching her like that.

'Libby, I can't do this,' he said harshly, the words like nails into her heart. 'I want to, of course I want to, but I'm not free.'

Libby felt as if the air had been sucked right out of her lungs. For a few moments neither of them moved, then her breath caught on a sob, breaking the spell, and abruptly, as if realising how suddenly improper and sordid their position was, he let her close her legs.

He helped the numbed hands she lifted automatically to rearrange her dress then waited a short time, his impassive eyes coolly observant, and she knew he saw everything—her pallor, her pain, her embarrassment and mostly her shame.

'You're married?' she demanded thickly.

'I've been in…a relationship,' he said huskily. 'We're…thinking about marriage. Her name is Paula. She's coming here for the weekend. She's probably on her way already.'

'You didn't tell me,' she whispered. 'If I'd known you had a girlfriend already, I'd never have… I didn't know.'

'I'm sorry.'

Libby tilted her chin, hurt beyond belief but not wanting him to guess just how desperately. 'Do you love her?'

He shook his head, not as if to deny it, but as if to suggest the question was irrelevant. 'We're well matched.'

'But if you're so sure then why…?' She lifted her arms helplessly. 'Why this? Why me?'

'Sex, Libby.' The word made her shiver uncontrollably, but he continued, still softly, 'You're enchanting. You're sweet and gentle and utterly desirable. I want you. I've wanted you from the first moment I saw you. Tonight I…lost control for a few minutes. After last week I never meant to touch you again. I never *should* have touched you.'

'Nathan, I'm in love with you—'

'No.' His hand covered her mouth, stopping the plea before she could voice it. 'Don't,' he ordered quietly. 'Trust me. I understand that you might think you feel that way but you don't. I've listened to you talk about your life. Outside of Alistair I'm probably the only man you've spent time with in two years. It's natural for you to feel this way now, but when I leave you'll start to understand that your feelings for me are shallow and temporary.

'I'm not right for you. You need to find someone your own age, someone who lives here—not someone like me far away in London who'd only want to drag you away from where you belong and ruin your life. I couldn't do that to you. If it's any consolation I'll never forgive myself for tonight.'

She sagged. He was wrong about her feelings being temporary and wrong to put her falling in love down simply to her not meeting many men. She loved him for how he was, for his warmth and his kindness and for the way he laughed and for the way she felt when he looked at her, and not out of desperation or loneliness because until now she'd never experienced either.

'Please, don't feel guilty. Nothing really happened,' she whispered when he lifted his head. 'You didn't even kiss me. Also, you've had almost a whole bottle of wine,' she heard herself saying. 'And I…well, I encouraged you. These things happen.'

If anything, her words, which had been intended to be comforting, seemed to make things worse, for him at least, because as he turned away she saw that his face was contorted with what looked like despair. He left without saying anything more, leaving the door to bang shut behind him, and she sagged against the wall, enveloped in her own lonely mist of misery.

Paula had never visited Cornwall before so the next afternoon Nathan drove her around the coast. It was a warm spring day, with only a very light breeze coming off the sea. After spending an hour or so strolling around the picturesque settlement of St Ives, they drove north and parked beside a beach near Newquay, watching agile surfers propelling themselves through the waves.

Paula shuddered. 'That water must be frigid. How on earth do they bear it?'

Nathan gave her a sideways look, hating himself for the sudden vision of Libby, rising gloriously naked from the sea. 'You don't like to swim?'

'There's swimming and there's swimming, darling.' She arched finely sculptured eyebrows. 'I don't object to warm and sandy beaches on the Mediterranean.' She sent him a telling look. 'If my little…false alarm hadn't been a false alarm we could have been planning a week on the Med for our honeymoon.'

Nathan sighed. 'I don't expect I'd have made a particularly good husband.'

'Nonsense.' Her impeccably scarlet mouth pouted at him. 'You're eminently suitable husband material.'

He winced. 'Sounds like a disease. Is that how you think of me?'

She laughed. 'Darling, that's exactly what you *are* and

I'm sure I'm not the first to tell you. You know I wouldn't say no, Nathan. Even without the baby. We're very suited.'

'Yes.' His gaze strayed to the water. 'I know. Give me some time to think about it, Paula.'

'Of course.' She leaned across and kissed him, brushing his thigh lightly with one long finger and letting it glide up as if to tease him, only it didn't tease him at all because his body failed to react. 'You're very grim today, darling,' she said throatily. 'You're making me quite excited. Shall we rush back to your little hideaway?'

Taking the anaesthetist back to the cottage, that was the last thing Nathan wanted to do yet, and to conceal his lack of response he lifted Paula's finger away and wrapped his hand around it. 'Later,' he said smoothly. 'Let's take a stroll around the village.'

He managed to delay returning to the bay until late that evening after a meal of superb seafood in a simple restaurant on the North Cornish coast. On the journey home he mentioned he was thinking about reducing his commitment to St Stephen's to part time and starting up his own practice.

Paula seemed delighted with the idea. Not surprising, he acknowledged, considering she'd been trying to coax him into private surgery for years. 'Darling, why not start up at the Leighton?' she said, referring to the private hospital where she already worked several sessions a week. 'The facilities are superb and, with Raymond's retirement, I'll have a spare day there. We could do a day list as well as another half day together.'

He lifted one shoulder. The idea of having her as his anaesthetist was appealing, provided he could make up his mind about leaving the NHS. 'The morality of private practice never worries you?'

She laughed, giving him a rather old-fashioned look. 'You have such quaint principles, Nathan. Private medicine is the way of the future and to be brutal, darling, just think about the money. I earn more in two days a week at the Leighton than I'd make in two weeks in the NHS if I was full time. Working as a team, we'll earn a fortune!'

He found her preoccupation with income distasteful but knew Paula well enough to accept that debating the point wouldn't assist either of them. Deliberately he changed the subject.

It was less easy to divert her from the subject of sex. 'Darling, what's wrong?' Soon after midnight she came into the study where he'd gone to work when she'd gone to bed. Her body beneath the transparent nightie she wore looked tense and impatient and her mouth was drawn into a pout. 'Aren't you ready for bed yet?'

'I have to finish this.' He lifted her hands away from where they'd lowered to his shoulders. 'I'm sorry, Paula. I'm going to be late tonight.'

'But, darling,' she protested, 'it's been over a month.'

'I'm sorry,' he repeated tightly, hating the need to make excuses, but, much as he would have preferred it, he could hardly ignore her. 'I'm stuck on something here. Don't wait. Last night I was up till dawn.' Brooding, not working, but that was hardly something he was going to share with Paula. 'I'll see you in the morning.'

'Goodnight, then.' The abrupt haughtiness of her expression suggested there would be a confrontation about this, but to his relief it seemed it would not be immediate because she spun around and left him alone.

He fell onto the couch about four in the morning and slept through until he woke to the sounds of running water, suggesting that Paula was already up and showering.

He got up, pulled on his jumper and went to make tea. The water shut off and he heard her moving into the bedroom and a little while later her heels on the floor behind him.

'Breakfast, darling?' Unexpectedly, when he'd been steeling himself for entirely justified anger, her voice was bright. 'How nice.' She surveyed the cereal and toast he'd laid out. 'Marmalade, too. Lovely.'

'I need a shower,' he said heavily, moving towards the door. 'After that, Paula, we need to talk.'

'No hurry.' She returned his dark look with a bland smile. 'Enjoy your shower, darling. I hope I haven't used all your hot water.'

She hadn't, but it wouldn't have mattered if she had because, after soaping, he turned the water to cold and held himself under the icy spray until it no longer stung. As soon as it stopped searing his flesh he swung the lever to 'Off' and stepped out.

There was no sign of Paula when he emerged from the bedroom, after pulling on jeans and a shirt. The breakfast dishes and tea were untouched, suggesting she'd not started eating. Not bothering with shoes, he wandered out into the garden. 'Paula?' But she wasn't there either.

He walked to the edge of the cliff, looked down at the beach and then swore. Paula was at the far side near a pile of driftwood—but she wasn't alone. He ran to the path and sprinted down, catching at small bushes either side of him for support as his feet slid in his haste.

As he ran along the beach he saw that Paula, her back to him, was talking to Libby, but Libby's head was lowered, as if she were being battered, and she couldn't see him. Her cats could, though. They stood on either side of their mistress, as if protecting her, but as he approached they seemed to relax their guard a little, their angry fur settling as they folded themselves down like two little sphinxes.

Both women seemed startled by his arrival, but Libby especially. She was in her swimming costume, a towel draped around her waist, and he could still see the firm, high shape of her breasts beneath the damp fabric. Her hair hung wet and sleek around her shoulders and down her back, and he felt his body respond involuntarily as he thought about burying himself in it and baring those breasts to his touch.

But while to him she still looked like the most beautiful creature on earth he could see she was upset, her face pale and strained. He looked grimly at Paula, wondering what she could have been saying to Libby to get her into such a state.

'Sorry, darling.' Paula stretched up and pressed a possessive kiss to his lips, one hand resting provocatively against his thighs and then stilling as she obviously became aware of his arousal. 'Were you missing me?'

He saw Libby's hastily lowered eyelids and felt sick.

Paula, though, was still talking. 'We've been introducing ourselves,' she announced, her eyes jerking between the two of them—him then Libby, him and Libby again, then back to him—accusingly, as if she suddenly understood something he'd never meant her to understand.

'You didn't tell me you had such a...fascinating neighbour.' When he said nothing she continued, 'Libby knows how to make all sorts of mysterious concoctions. Her grandmother taught her. I asked her to make me a love potion but then I remembered how passionate you can be.' Once again her fingers brushed against the fastenings of his jeans. 'And I realised that I don't really need one, do I, darling?'

'Paula, don't.' He took her hand away and held her by the wrist, knowing this was all going horribly wrong, but his concern was for Libby. 'Libby, are you all right?'

'A slight headache,' she said faintly, one slim hand rising vaguely to her temple, and he had to force himself not to reach for her to comfort her.

'Oh, dear.' Perhaps sensing his worry, Paula sounded anything but concerned. 'You'd better get out of the sun.'

Nathan glared at her briefly, before looking back to Libby. She looked shaken and unbelievably frail. 'I'll help you home,' he said quietly.

'No!' Libby stretched out one small arm as if to fend him off, and he flinched from the real fear he could see in her eyes. 'It's not that bad.'

'In that case we'll leave you to it,' Paula said crisply. 'Come along, Nathan.' She tucked her arm into his elbow. 'Don't bully the child.'

Was that what he'd been doing? Libby avoided his eyes, bending to pick up one of her cats. 'I'll be fine,' she said, her voice muffled by the creature's fur. 'Enjoy your day.'

'Oh, we will,' drawled Paula, 'even if I can't drag Nathan out of the bedroom again.'

Nathan's brows drew together harshly. For a short moment he was too stunned to think of any response, but in the meantime Paula said smoothly, 'Darling, don't be such a prude. Libby's old enough to know about the birds and the bees.' Her gaze sharpened pointedly. 'Just.'

He felt his skin flush. 'You've said enough,' he said grimly, seeing that Libby looked almost about to collapse. He knew he had to get the older woman away from her. 'Libby, I'm sorry,' he muttered harshly, but if she heard him she didn't react, merely turning away from them both to look out towards the sea as Nathan tugged Paula towards the path.

She waited until they were back in the cottage. 'Well, well, darling.' She sent him a cold smile. 'How intriguing. You are a dark horse. A holiday romance. She is dangerously young, though. Do you think this could be your mid-life crisis?'

Nathan winced. 'I haven't touched her,' he countered wearily. 'Not the way you're thinking.'

'Darling, it's blindingly obvious you want to.'

He leaned back against the wall and closed his eyes briefly. 'Paula…'

'Oh, no apologies, Nathan.' She gave a mock shudder. 'Please, no. No soul-baring or anguish. Let's keep this civilised. Far be it from me to advise you how to live your life, but lucky for both of us that I persuaded you to let me come down, don't you think?'

She strode into the bedroom and he followed her, watching while she collected her cosmetics and toiletries. 'I'm sure if I'd been pregnant you'd have behaved honourably, but, happily, now you don't need to.' She zipped up her bag then straightened with another of her cool smiles. 'Nothing to say?'

'Only that I'm sorry.' Even if she didn't want an apology, she deserved one. 'You don't have to leave, Paula. You wanted a weekend away so stay.' Until the day before he'd still been thinking there was a chance she was pregnant so he'd planned to drive her up on Monday night himself, leaving his own car for the local garage to transport. 'We'll go exploring somewhere, have a meal. I'll use the other bedroom tonight.'

'I don't think so, darling.' She patted his cheek on her way past. 'You're looking quite strained,' she observed. 'Must be all those raging hormones. Better sleep with the girl at least once. Knowing men the way I do, I expect that's the only way you'll get her out of your system.'

Nathan gritted his teeth. He collected her bag, reached ahead of her to open the front door, then followed her out to her car. When she'd opened the boot he deposited her bag inside, closed it and came around to her door, holding it open while she slid into the driver's seat.

'I'll still marry you, Nathan.' She seemed amused by his numb look. 'If you ask me. After your holiday when you're back in London and over this little…adventure of yours.

I'm a very practical woman, you see, and you're a little too tempting to give up easily. Think about it, darling.'

Nathan felt his face harden. He shut her door with barely constrained force. 'Drive safely, Paula.'

CHAPTER EIGHT

AFTER Nathan left with the woman she knew he was probably going to marry, Libby folded herself into a small, forlorn package and sank to the ground, one hand automatically stroking Duncan as she stared blindly out to sea.

Later, much later, Nathan dropped William onto the sand beside her. 'He came to fetch me,' he said quietly. He sat beside her, his knees bent. 'Libby, I'm sorry.'

'Your fiancée's very beautiful.' She lifted dry, gritty eyes towards the path. 'Have you set a date?'

'No.' He lifted one shoulder as if he was uncertain. 'At this moment I don't even want to think about Paula, but in the future…? When I'm back in my normal life…? The truth is, Libby, I don't know what's going to happen.'

'Have you left her at the cottage?'

'She's gone back to London.' He sighed, the strained lines around his eyes deepening. 'And I'm sorry she came down to the beach. I didn't mean that to happen. You weren't supposed to meet her.'

Libby released Duncan so he could follow his brother towards the path, watching the tiny pawprints he left in the pebbly sand. 'She didn't like me.'

'No.' He leaned back on his elbows, looking at the water. 'Forget her.'

She almost smiled at that. He had no idea. 'I didn't say anything bad,' she said quickly, looking at him in sudden appeal, wanting him to understand that she'd not told the woman anything, not mentioned the night before. 'I don't understand why she was so angry—'

But he didn't let her finish, his voice interrupting, 'She was angry with me, Libby. Not you.'

'But why would she be angry with you?' she argued. 'I didn't say anything about you.'

'You didn't have to *say* anything. Libby, even you can't be that naïve. She could see how I reacted to you.' As if he'd sensed her uncertainty he took her hand and dragged it to his groin. 'Feel, Libby, feel what you do to me.'

She snatched her hand away, shocked by his hardness, and his voice gentled. 'You see, it's not your fault,' he said distantly. 'It's mine.'

'But—'

'But nothing.' He sat up again, his hands clenching on his knees. 'I told you last night I wanted you. If you weren't such an innocent you'd have known from the beginning.'

Libby's thoughts were turning to a jumbled mass that made her head ache anew, but one thing flew clear. He wanted her. And, yes, he'd told her that the night before as well so it had to be true. Even if he was in love with his Paula, he wanted her, Libby. 'W-what did she say?'

'Paula thinks you're my mid-life crisis.'

She felt hot colour sear her face, saw his impassive gaze register the blush and felt her colour deepen. 'You're too young.'

'I disagree.' His shoulder lifted coolly. 'I think she's probably right.'

She forced herself to meet his eyes, knowing that he'd read all the secret longings in hers but no longer caring. 'Does she want you to leave?'

'On the contrary,' he said flatly. 'Her advice was to sleep with you. In her opinion it's the only way I'll get you out of my system.'

Libby's heart thudded dangerously. Shaking, she turned onto her side, away from him, hugging her knees to her chest. 'So are you going to? Sleep with me, I mean?'

'Isn't that up to you?'

He'd spoken quietly, his voice so deep it made her shiver. 'I think I would like that,' she whispered. Even knowing he'd go from her to Paula wasn't enough to change that.

'Libby, you're very young—'

'I'm an adult woman, Nathan.' She'd never felt so adult, and when she felt him move beside her, when his hands came to her shoulders and drew her gently back against his chest so that she sat in front of him, their legs bent together, the thundering of her heart was so loud she had to strain to hear him.

'What about Alistair?' he murmured, his mouth bent to her ear.

She closed her eyes weakly. 'Alistair's a dear friend,' she told him, 'but no matter what he said to you he's not in love with me. There's nothing between us.'

'He told me to be kind to you,' he murmured, his fingers tightening just fractionally on her as if this was difficult for him. 'He called you the love of his life.'

'That's just him,' she said softly. 'Always joking. You know how he is. He likes cool blondes,' she added, her heart contracting coldly as she realised that, judging from his girlfriend, Nathan shared his brother's preferences. 'Haven't you noticed?'

'Tastes change,' he said simply.

Libby didn't know how to convince him. 'He's never tried to kiss me or touch me,' she insisted, tilting her head back so she could look at him. 'He's never said anything. I've known him for two years. Don't you think I would have realised if he was interested?'

His eyes narrowed. 'You didn't know with me,' he said quietly.

She flushed. 'Alistair's less…inscrutable.'

'Inscrutable?' His hand slid beneath the swimsuit fabric

she'd replaced and, covering her breast, he tugged her back hard against him, his eyes narrowing as she caught her breath in response to the incredible intimacy of his touch. 'Hardly.'

She swallowed, feeling as if she might die if he stopped caressing her. Abruptly he turned, spinning her so she lay face down on the sand beneath him. 'I don't love you,' he said quietly, stressing the words as if it was vitally important she understood. 'At least not in any way that's good for you.'

'I know that.'

His hands slid beneath her, capturing her breasts again, the rasping friction of the sand on his hands almost driving her insane. 'You don't know what you do to me,' he said hoarsely. For a few minutes they lay there, still, and then suddenly he levered himself away and hauled her up. His eyes faintly dazed, he tucked her arm back into her strap, covering her again. He tugged her hand. 'Come up to the cottage.'

'No!' Libby recoiled. She couldn't let it happen there, not where he'd been with the other woman.

His mouth twisted as if he sensed the reason for her sudden horror, but his glance at the beach was rueful. 'Not here, Libby,' he said quietly. 'Not now.'

'My cottage, then.' It seemed absurd, this formal little discussion about practicalities, considering the enormity of what they were about to do, but she found herself dwelling on it. 'It's only a single bed but it's not the very smallest type.'

'Sweet Libby.' Carefully he tucked her hair behind her ears, his gaze tender.

She took one of his hands, twisting her mouth to kiss it, and he draped one arm around her waist. They walked slowly up the path. At the top he hesitated, his eyes shadowed again. 'I have to go next door for a few minutes. It's not too late to change your mind.'

She swallowed heavily. 'Please, come back.'

She didn't want to go inside, couldn't go inside without him, so she waited on her porch, sitting on the step, hugging her knees to her chest, her mind half-numb.

He wasn't long. His face was tight, controlled even, and if she hadn't known him better she'd have thought him nervous. He offered her his hand to help her stand up. Despite the tenseness of his expression, his eyes were kind, and she felt some of her strain ease. 'I need a drink,' he said gently. 'Make me some of your horrible tea?'

She managed a small smile. 'Yes,' she said quietly, feeling a sudden thirst for some camomile to soothe her nerves. 'I'll bring it out.'

But, instead of waiting on the porch, he followed her inside. 'Have you met many of Alistair's girlfriends?' he asked.

She looked up sharply from where she was filling the kettle, startled by the question. 'Four or five, I suppose, over the years. Haven't you?'

He didn't answer, merely tilted his head. 'Anyone serious?'

'I don't think so.' She tucked her hair behind her ears, shaking her head. 'He seems to enjoy playing the field.'

'Do you find him attractive?' he asked abruptly.

She put the kettle on to boil, before answering. 'I'd have to say yes,' she admitted. 'He's very good-looking.' As Nathan's face darkened she rushed on. 'But that doesn't mean I'm attracted to him,' she said quickly. 'Nathan, we've talked about this already. There's nothing between us.'

He leaned against the bench, his arms crossed, watching her broodingly. 'If he does prove to be interested, could there be something between you in the future?'

And find herself faced with Nathan and his wife at every family occasion? Leaving aside the thought that no relationship with Alistair could ever come close to the intensity of what she experienced with Nathan, the thought was unbearable. 'Never.'

He seemed to relax at that, the worried creases beside his eyes fading fractionally, and she realised he'd been afraid of what might happen. Obviously he'd be worried that if she became involved with his brother it might lead to friction within the family.

Libby swallowed heavily. 'I'll never tell him,' she said huskily, sensing from the almost guilty way he looked away that she'd guessed correctly.

But his verbal reply was strong, and she wondered if she'd been wrong after all. 'Tell him what you want.' He braced his arms on the bench, leaning forward slightly as if to stretch them. 'It's not going to make any difference.'

'Here's your tea,' she said carefully, lowering his cup to the bench beside him. 'Do you want lunch? A sandwich?'

'Nothing.' He lifted the cup and tasted the hot liquid experimentally, grimacing only very faintly before taking several mouthfuls.

They drank in silence, but it was a tense, awkward silence, and Libby was conscious of a slowly rising dread that, instead of staying with her, he would leave. Once, twice, she opened her mouth to ask him, but he looked preoccupied with his own thoughts and she left him to them.

When they'd finished she took his cup, then turned away, rinsing them clean. 'Nathan, there's something I haven't told you,' she said finally, staring out at the cliffs rather than back towards him. 'I mean, I know last night and before on the beach I might have seemed a little... immodest, but I've never...I mean with you this will be the first time I've ever—'

'It's all right, Libby. I know.' He sounded almost amused by her hesitant explanation, but when she turned quickly to look at him his expression was unreadable.

She felt her head drop a little. He'd definitely changed his mind, she thought tensely when he didn't move. He didn't want her any more.

She turned back to the dishes but then she heard his chair shift and seconds later his arms slid around her waist and she sagged weakly with relief.

'Your hair's still damp,' he muttered hoarsely, nuzzling the side of her head. He shifted the heavy strands away, his mouth seeking her neck. He licked gently at her skin, then bit very softly, holding her body as she arched against him. 'You taste of salt.'

Libby's head tipped back. 'I need to shower it off.'

'Mmm.' He bent and swung her into his arms and she pressed tiny brave kisses to his throat as he carried her to her bathroom. He switched on the water and, without waiting for it to warm, carried her immediately beneath the spray, laughing at her shrieks as the cold shocked her out of the delicious languor his nearness had induced.

'It's good for you,' he mocked, lowering her but blocking off her exit with the bulk of his body, catching the urgent hands she lifted to the control lever. 'Enjoy it.'

But it was freezing, worse even than the sea, yet although she struggled she found herself laughing, too, for while she at least was in her swimsuit, he was fully dressed and almost as drenched. She used the arms he raised to hold her to haul him forward against her directly under the water. 'You enjoy it,' she cried in triumph.

'I'm about to.' He pressed her against the wall of the cubicle, ignoring the water to plunder her willing mouth. Gradually, frustratingly slowly, he kissed her, again and again, and when he lifted his head, his face darkly shadowed, he was breathing as quickly as she, and the water was warm and the cubicle so full of steam she could see nothing but him. He left her, hushing her protests with another drugging kiss, and within seconds he was back, naked, and she caught her breath at the potent male power of his desire.

He reached for her again, two lingering kisses that made her head spin, then he drew away so he stood just outside the shower. 'Undress for me, Libby,' he muttered hoarsely, lifting her hands to her straps. 'Show me.'

But she was still shy and she hesitated, not knowing how to please him, but although he no longer touched her his attention was riveted on her skin above her suit and she was encouraged. Slowly she eased the straps off her arm. 'Good girl,' he whispered, so quietly she could only just hear him above the water.

When she bared her breasts he groaned. 'More, Libby. Don't stop. I want to see all of you.'

But once her stomach was uncovered her courage deserted her and she faltered, looking up at him pleadingly. As if sensing her fear, he was immediately back with her, gathering her into his arms, his mouth lowering passionately. 'You're so beautiful,' he muttered against her lips. 'I've never known any woman so beautiful.'

This time as he kissed her he soaped her, his hands gliding silkily across her back, her breasts, her abdomen, gently, very gently, easing down her suit, lifting her so he could slide it clear of her legs.

Still kissing her, his hands caressed the skin he'd bared, and when his soapy fingers slid between her thighs the room seemed to spin and she gasped, leaning back against the wall. 'Nathan,' she whispered urgently, not understanding what was happening to her.

'Relax.' He lifted her, supporting her against the wall as his mouth lowered to her breast. 'Let me. Just relax.'

But it was impossible to relax and her head twisted from

side to side as she clutched at his shoulders made slippery by the steaming water. The maddening tug of his mouth at her nipples suckled at the remains of her reservations, but it was the delicate, insistent pressure of his soapy hand that made her breath come in hoarse gasps until the mindless spasm of unbelievable pleasure flooded across her body, robbing her of thought and breath.

She collapsed against him, shivering, aching and breathless. Dimly she was aware of him lifting her upright, and then she knew he was washing her again, soaping her, his fingers infinitely gentle now, comforting not arousing. She heard the water stop, felt herself enveloped in a soft towel and then knew he was carrying her into her bedroom.

As though through a fog, Libby realised that he was caressing her again. She could feel her weary body responding to his hands but it was as if it was happening to someone else, far away. Vaguely she was aware of the few seconds he left her and then he returned, gently parting her thighs before sliding himself into her languid heat. There was no pain, just the wet abrasion of him as he moved deep within her, then she heard the hoarse cry that was her name before he collapsed above her.

Libby wrapped him in her arms, smiling, and her body drifted into sleep.

She woke to the delicate tug of his mouth at her breast. When she stirred he lifted his head, his face shadowed in the remains of the day's light that penetrated the room. 'Hello, sleepyhead. Good rest?'

It felt as if her whole body were flushing as she met his amused gaze. 'I—I'm sorry,' she stammered, hardly knowing where to look. 'I didn't realise I was so tired.'

He laughed softly, brushing her hot cheek with one gentle hand. 'I didn't mind,' he said easily, lowering his head back to her breast. 'I kept myself busy.'

She closed her eyes, catching her breath at his touch. 'You must be hungry,' she said faintly.

He rolled above her, supporting himself on his elbows. 'Are you?'

She shook her head, her mouth drying as she acknowledged that it wasn't food she wanted. 'No.'

'Neither am I.' He kissed her gently on the mouth, then again more forcibly. 'I want to make love with you, Libby. Right now.'

She entwined her legs around him, pulling him even closer. 'Me, too,' she whispered shyly.

He laughed again. 'You brazen hussy,' he teased, brushing aside her hair so he could circle her peaked nipple with his tongue. 'You're shameless.'

She lifted herself into his mouth, gripping his hair to hold him against her. 'Don't stop,' she said breathlessly, feeling the pressure begin to rise again as he rocked forward.

But he hushed her, leaning across to fetch something from the floor beside the bed. 'Not just yet,' he said softly when she moaned a protest as he untangled himself from her. He undid the little packet and covered himself, and within seconds was taking her back in his arms. 'Always that first,' he said gently, as he probed her softness.

As he penetrated her she felt her body close around him, rejoiced in the hoarse groan that told her he felt it too.

This time when she felt the spasm she arched up, her scream, a muffled cry against his shoulder, mingling with his gasp so that they fell together, breathless and hot, into a drained and dreamless sleep.

She woke once during the night to feel him close against her back, and they made love again, a slow, languid coupling that seemed to last hours before they once again slept.

Nathan woke very early, around five, enmeshed in Libby's beautiful hair. For an hour or so he just watched her sleep, enjoying the chance to study her openly. Her face was a perfect oval, her skin soft and creamy with a smattering of enchanting freckles across her small nose, her lashes long and sooty against her pale cheek, but it wasn't her beauty that moved him. It was what he'd see if she opened her eyes—that shy, mysterious, yet vulnerable look that bewitched him, captivated him so that he wanted to discover everything about her.

For one thing was overwhelmingly clear. Despite Paula's casual reference to sleeping with Libby, one night with her hadn't been enough. One night with her and he still ached just from looking at her. One night and he desired more, immediately.

He flicked the corner of her mouth with his tongue, catching his breath at the obedient way it opened to him. 'Wake up, sweet,' he murmured, lowering his hand to graze her nipple, his thighs tautening as it, too, responded to his touch. 'It's morning.'

Later he returned to Alistair's to shower and change, joining Libby an hour later for breakfast. She looked happy, he decided, assessing her shy, smiling eyes, the faint colour in her cheeks when she looked at him and the languid grace of her movements. He found himself gratified by that, although, he told himself fiercely, he hadn't done anything any reasonably experienced man couldn't have done for her.

She'd have been better off with another man, he acknowledged grimly, knowing that whatever she'd said she wouldn't find it easy dealing with the end of this relationship. She was too fragile, too easily hurt, he thought, hating the part of him that urged him to ignore that.

But there was no going back now and even if he'd wanted to he was too weak to stop himself reaching for her again when he already ached for her.

She was carrying their plates towards the sink, and as

she turned sideways to him the sunlight filtered through her blouse, showing him the lifting curve of her bare breast beneath the fabric, and he felt his fists clench against the table. His thighs tautened. 'Libby?'

At his husky command she turned around and he saw first surprise then pleasure in her expression, and the pleasure moved him immeasurably. In a single, smooth movement she lifted the blouse over her head. Although her hair covered her breasts, his breathing locked as he acknowledged the quiet female confidence in the gesture, a confidence that belied the nervous lift of her breathing and the flush of her cheeks.

In that moment he would have given her anything in the world that she wanted but he had only himself. Wordlessly he collected her in his arms and carried her back to the bedroom.

Later that day they went for a walk, first along the beach then up to the cliffs on the other side and along a grassy path that took them along a few bays. Now and again they stopped and kissed and, conscious of a strong need to keep her close, he held her small hand firmly entwined with his as they followed the track.

It was cooler today and they were now both wearing jeans and wool jumpers. As the afternoon wore on the wind, which had been fresh to start with, began to gust harder. He smiled as Libby lifted her face appreciatively at one particularly strong gust in open delight at the fresh sea smell and the faint salty spray against her face. 'Wonderful,' she cried, her enchanting green eyes sparkling as her hair flew back in the gusty wind like a dark, silky sail. 'Don't you love it like this?'

Nathan laughed, catching her to him in a rough embrace. 'You're insane,' he murmured against her sweet mouth. 'Normal people like calm weather.'

At the third bay along they took a path which led down

to the beach. By now, although the sea was rough and noisy, it was low tide and so they wandered back along the sand, scrambling over rocks. Sometimes at an impassable stretch they had to climb back to the cliffs but then they simply returned to the beach as soon as they could.

The increasingly wild wind and the hard pounding of the water made it an exhilarating walk, and he realised they were both delaying their return to the relative shelter of the cottages. It felt as if the longer they waited, the greater the pleasure would be when they finally came together again.

They lingered at rock pools, toying playfully with colourful sea anemones and shells. He teased her with a small wriggling crab, threatening to toss it up her jumper, although in reality—far from wanting to throw the creature up at her—he'd only lifted her jumper so he could look at her breasts again.

Instead of running from him, she let him look, her eyes dancing as she saw his weakness, then, pouting, she rescued the little animal from him and replaced it carefully in the sand. He hugged her to him, laughing at her expression. 'I wasn't going to hurt him,' he said huskily. 'He just wanted to see you.'

By the time they finally got back the clouds had closed in, menacingly dark, drowning out the last hours of daylight, and the wind was high and wild. He chased her up the path from the beach, lifting and loosening and tugging at her clothes each time he caught her so by the time they reached her cottage she was weak with laughter and nearly bared to him.

Aroused beyond belief Nathan almost took her there, on the floor, in the kitchen, her soft pleas driving him close to insane with the desire to pleasure her, but he couldn't protect her here. Somehow he found the strength to grip some stray vestige of control, containing himself long enough to carry her to the bedroom.

*   *   *

Monica's blue eyes were shrewdly assessing when Libby showed her into her workroom the next afternoon. 'I want whatever you've been taking,' she said bluntly. 'You're blooming.'

Libby felt herself flush. 'Fresh air and exercise,' she said crisply, glad Monica was undressing behind the screen and unable to see her embarrassment. 'I've been doing a lot of walking.'

Monica's eyebrows arched sceptically when she reappeared. 'So that's why you didn't object to me postponing yesterday.' She slid onto the bench. 'You wanted a little exercise.'

'That's right,' Libby confirmed as she mixed her oils.

'Been seeing Nathan?' the older woman asked boldly, as Libby lowered the sheet in preparation for massaging her arms. 'You know we thought he was incredibly sexy—'

'That's enough, Monica.' Libby, not wanting the conversation to continue one more moment, put on her firmest professional face. 'Relax, now. Close your eyes.'

After Monica, Libby busied herself in her garden, weeding and tidying up the damage from the storm the night before. Fortunately most of the property was sheltered by either stone walls or the hedge and so it was only the exposed plants at the back of her collection in the centre of the lawn, her rosemary, comfrey, and fennel, that needed much attention.

Now and again she glanced through the hedge towards Alistair's cottage. The knowledge that Nathan was inside, working, didn't help her keep her mind on her task. She rocked back on her heels. Nor did knowing it would be hours before she saw him again.

After breakfast he'd told her very firmly that he had to spend the day working, and although his departure had been gratifyingly reluctant she hadn't been brave enough to interrupt him even to offer him lunch.

Although she knew him intimately now, and her mouth dried at the thought of how very intimately that meant, there was still a barrier between them, a barrier he'd erected and now seemed determined to maintain. Physically, over these past two nights they could have been no closer, but emotionally she understood him now no better than she had before they'd made love. Even as they'd lain, exhausted, in each other's arms he'd remained hidden to her.

Absently she patted William, who'd come to see what she was doing, wondering if Nathan was different with Paula. She winced at the memory of the cool, elegant woman who'd made her feel like an ignorant child that day on the beach. However much she longed to seize these precious days, ignoring all else, to pretend he didn't love another woman would give rise to wild foolish dreams that would do her only harm.

Viciously she pulled out a tiny weed that had entangled its roots amongst her vervain. Did *she* know him? Did he ever lose that tight control with *her*? Did *she* ever have the satisfaction of knowing she'd driven him to the edge of sanity the way he could push her, Libby, so far she thought she might break free of her body and fly away?

Or, more disturbingly because above all she loved him and wanted him happy, did this…shield he held around himself keep out even the woman he loved?

'You look thoughtful.'

Libby's head snapped up and she blushed as she met Nathan's knowing eyes. 'I—I didn't hear you,' she stammered, straightening quickly to greet him, brushing her shorts free of grass. He looked wonderful to her, dark and inscrutable and very male, unbearably handsome in his jeans and crisp, pale shirt. She shivered with the unbelievable thought that temporarily, at least, he was hers. 'I thought you were working.'

'My mind wandered.' He didn't look pleased, though,

his mouth compressing almost impatiently as he reached for her. 'I missed you,' he muttered against her cheek, the rawness in his voice suggesting he'd made the admission unwillingly. 'Your mouth,' he murmured, and then he kissed her. 'And your breasts,' he added, his hands sliding beneath her top to close around her for one brief hungry moment. Ignoring her groaned protest, he released her body but, instead of leaving, he took her hand and tugged her towards her cottage, his eyes darkly intent.

His desire when she knew he'd wanted to work gave her confidence and this time, instead of letting him lead her, it was she who drew him into her bedroom. Then slowly, concentrating, she undressed him, ducking away from his seeking hands until he gave up and let her do what she wanted.

Laughing, she forced him to lie still while she took her time undressing, removing each layer piece by piece, folding her clothes neatly before turning to the next, shielding herself with her hair because she knew that that, above all, teased him.

Dizzy with her daring and the knowledge of his arousal, she straddled him, letting her breasts brush his mouth as she stretched for one of the little packets he'd left near the bed and then lifting herself away from his eager mouth so she could unroll the protection over him, imitating the way she'd seen him do it.

His groan as his hands clenched her buttocks, urging her against him, weakened her resolve, though, and not able to delay any longer she lifted herself and rocked forward onto him, her movements no longer smooth but urgent and demanding, not caring about power or control but only about the steadily increasing pressure between them.

For the first time she felt him tense before her, felt him tremble beneath her, felt a moment of sheer triumph, but instead of stilling he arched, pulling her down and tumbling her under him, urgently bringing her to a shuddering release, her hoarse cries muffled against his shoulder as he surged within her.

As she lay sweating and panting beside him she knew she'd failed. Even at that moment of absolute pleasure when he'd risen, flushed and intense before her, she'd seen his control, his consideration, and had known he hadn't abandoned himself to her. Libby, all too aware of her own absolute surrender, felt helplessly inadequate and she turned her head aside, her eyes closing weakly.

As always, he was too sensitive. 'Libby…?' One lazy arm wrapped itself around her waist and dragged her back against him. His mouth nuzzled her ear. 'What's wrong?'

'Nothing,' she said faintly, knowing there was no way she could ever explain. It barely made sense to her. He'd given her unimaginable pleasure—she could hardly tell him she'd have preferred to be neglected.

But he rolled her back, his eyes concerned as they ran down her body. 'Did I hurt you?'

'Of course not.' She deliberately unclenched her fists. 'You were wonderful,' she whispered. 'Hold me.'

He lowered his mouth to her breast but she dragged him up again, frightened she might cry. 'Just hold me,' she ordered softly, turning back into his arms.

CHAPTER NINE

SOME time in the next week or so Nathan told Libby he'd be leaving the following Sunday, and when he woke her two mornings before he was due to go she knew he wanted to talk. But it would be about him leaving and, wanting to delay the pain as long as she could, she avoided him and pretended she was going to be busy that morning although in reality there was only Isabel Spalding and one other client to see.

Isabel's ulcer was healed now so that she didn't really need to come any more, but she seemed anxious not to lose contact yet, as if frightened that one missed visit might mean her leg opening up again, and Libby was happy to take the time to reassure her.

Her other client drew up just as she was helping Isabel into her husband's car in the lane, and once the elderly couple had departed Libby went to greet her.

The last time Dorothy Penrose had come to see her professionally had been more than a year earlier for help with her chronic eczema after her GP had suggested a trial of natural treatment instead of the steroid creams he'd been prescribing for years.

Dorothy hadn't been keen initially—it had taken Geoffrey months to persuade her to even talk to Libby— but the results had been convincing enough to turn her into a herbal enthusiast. 'It's back, is it?' Libby asked sympathetically, remembering how the older woman had suffered with itching. 'I'm very sorry.'

'It's not the eczema,' Dorothy said tightly, coming with her towards the cottage. 'It's this wretched indigestion.' She was holding one fist clenched near the top of her breast-bone. 'I've always had a bit of it but never like this. It's been bad for two weeks now. Nothing seems to work. Jim's brought me all sorts of things from the chemist and I've been taking that peppermint stuff like water but…nothing seems to be helping. It's just come on now again when I climbed out of the Land Rover. I only had tea for breakfast. I was hoping that meant I'd be all right.'

Worried by her pallor, Libby guided her into her work-room. 'What does Geoffrey say?'

'I didn't want to…bother him,' Dorothy said jerkily. 'After all the performance of taking those useless creams he gave me all those years, I'd rather take something natural.' With Libby's help she got up onto the couch. 'I mean, I can barely eat at the moment from fear of bringing on the pain. Another week of this and I'll have lost a stone at least. Is there anything you can…recommend?'

'Dorothy, I'm sorry but I don't want to give you anything without you having seen Geoffrey first.' Automatically her nursing instincts had made her check the older woman's pulse. It was a little fast but still reassuringly regular and strong. 'Tell me about the pain.'

'Normal indigestion pain,' Dorothy said grittily. 'It's not my heart if that's what you're worried about.'

Her heart was exactly what Libby *was* worried about. 'You don't look well.'

'If I could just get rid of the pain—'

'How often are you getting it?'

'I've had a bit occasionally for years but like this it started off just…now and then but this last week it feels like it's every time I move,' she said thickly. 'This is the second bout this morning. I should have got Jim to drive me only he's out on the farm this morning—' She broke off. 'You know I'm starting to feel quite…faint with it.'

'Rest back.' Libby eased her against the bed and lowered

the back of it. Checking her pulse again, she realised it felt weaker than it had a few minutes earlier. 'Dorothy, stay there,' she said urgently. 'I'm going to call Geoffrey to come and have a look at you.'

But before she could get to the phone Dorothy closed her eyes, drew one shuddering breath and then collapsed back into the bed, one arm falling limply over the edge.

Her heart pounding, Libby rushed back to the bed. She adjusted the back of it so that Dorothy lay flat, checked for a pulse in her neck, and when she found none she ran to the window, threw it open and shouted for Nathan.

If he didn't come she'd have to call for an ambulance herself, but in the meantime she tilted Dorothy's head back, checked with a sweep of her finger that her airway was clear and started CPR.

Nathan came running in seconds later. 'Libby…?'

'She's arrested,' she explained breathlessly, counting out her chest compressions between syllables. 'Call 999. See if they can send the helicopter.'

Her fifteen compressions up, she moved swiftly around to administer two quick breaths into Dorothy's mouth, before returning to her compressions.

Nathan was through to someone and over the pounding of her own heart Libby heard him describe the emergency and give the address. 'We're a nurse and doctor,' he was saying grimly. 'We'll try and keep her going until someone gets here.'

Libby moved back to give two more breaths as Nathan came over to the bed. 'The helicopter's on another job. They're sending an ambulance.' He hauled off his jumper and positioned the heel of one hand on the lower part of Dorothy's breastbone, waiting for her to finish. 'Any response?'

'No pulse yet,' she said breathlessly, her fingers feeling for where the carotid should have been.

Between groups of breaths she described for him what had happened. The wait for the ambulance seemed endless. From time to time they changed positions to give Nathan a rest, and she took over the compressions while he did mouth-to-mouth, but even her arms were aching by the time they heard the siren in the lane.

After that things moved fast. The ambulance was equipped with a defibrillator and oxygen and drugs, and Libby moved out of the way to let in one of the officers, who promptly slid an airway into Dorothy's mouth, covered that with a mask and started pumping in oxygen.

As soon as they'd arrived Nathan had quickly explained who he was, and now he took control of the defibrillator paddles while the other ambulance officer positioned himself to take over the chest compressions if more were required.

'Clear,' Nathan said briskly, so that they all drew back, and he shocked his patient.

He repeated the shock a few seconds later, and again at a higher voltage and then once more, nodding between each time for the ambulance officers to restart CPR. After the final shock he lifted his hand to stop them and Libby craned forward and saw on the defibrillator's monitor that a normal-looking, if slow cardiac trace had emerged.

'I've got a pulse,' the officer looking after Dorothy's airway said triumphantly, and Libby sagged against her work bench, weak with relief as she saw Dorothy's chest lift as she took a breath on her own.

The other ambulance officer had produced an intravenous cannula but he looked as if he was having trouble finding a vein and so, collecting herself, Libby wrapped her hands around Dorothy's forearm, tourniquet-style, trying to make the vessels stand out for him.

Nathan, in the meantime, was sorting through the drugs the officers had brought. 'I'll come with you into Truro,' he said calmly. 'Libby, see if you can get hold of the family.'

As soon as the officer had his line in place Libby went for the phone. But Dorothy's husband didn't answer. 'He's not there,' she told Nathan. With weak relief she saw that, while Dorothy's eyes were still closed, beneath the oxygen mask she was starting to stir. 'He's probably out on the farm. I'll drive up myself and try and find him.'

Nathan, connecting her cannula to a bag of fluid as the other two moved Dorothy onto their stretcher, merely gave her a preoccupied nod.

Jim Penrose was in his barn. She gently explained what had happened and drove him into Truro, delivering him into the hands of the kind-faced nurse who came to meet them at the entrance to the intensive care unit. 'The doctors are still with her now but she's conscious and stable at present,' she reassured them.

'Dr Thomas left just a minute or two ago,' the nurse added to Libby, when Libby explained who she was. It took her a few seconds to realise that the nurse was talking about Nathan. 'He said something about calling a taxi. If you run you might catch him outside before he finds one.'

But Nathan had beaten her. A taxi, coming the other way, passed her just before she turned into the lane, and Nathan was waiting for her at the cottage. 'I drove Jim to the hospital,' she said breathlessly, the words tumbling out of her as she hurried into his arms, needing him to hold her. 'He was so shaky he could barely walk. I must have just missed you.'

'I thought that might have been what had happened when you weren't here.' He hugged her back as hard as she needed him to. 'I think she's going to be all right. If she gets through the next twenty-four hours I'll be more certain, but she was talking when I left.'

'I don't want to go through that again.' She'd told him

about Jim shaking, but she was trembling just as badly herself now. 'I was so sure we were going to lose her. Thank heavens you were here.'

'You weren't doing too badly on your own.' Smiling, he drew back. 'You were very impressive, Nurse Deane. She couldn't have been in better hands. If I hadn't been here you'd have been able to keep her alive until the ambulance arrived.'

Libby hoped that was true. 'Well, obviously I know CPR,' she admitted. 'I've had to do it loads of times before. But it's not the same when it happens outside the hospital. When I used to be on the wards and Casualty, people used to collapse all the time. It used to be routine almost. We used to know what to do and we'd just get on and do it, only we were detached somehow because we had drugs and oxygen and airways and lots of doctors around. But the way it was today was...so shocking. So real. It was just us and Dorothy. Look.' She held out her hand so he could see. 'I can't stop shaking now. I can still feel the adrenaline floating around in my blood. I'd make a pretty stressed-out sort of nurse now.'

'You're being too hard on yourself.' Nathan smiled against her mouth as he kissed her. 'You're a fine nurse, Libby. You're just feeling the strain because you're not used to being in the front line any more.'

'She thought it was indigestion,' she murmured, between kisses. 'I was worried about her heart and it must have been angina.'

'Growing more unstable,' he agreed, covering her mouth. 'You're hot.'

'I know.' She let him unbutton her shirt, her own hands busy at his. 'I've been rushing. Take me to bed,' she whispered. 'Now, Nathan, please. I need to feel you.'

She had so many questions, so many thoughts, so much

need to talk through with him that night about what had happened that there was no thought of anything else.

But in the morning when she woke beside him she remembered that this was their last full day together and the knowledge was like a physical pain inside her chest.

Still not ready to talk, after they'd rung the hospital and discovered that Dorothy's blood tests had confirmed that she'd had a heart attack but that she was making steady and good progress, Libby sent Nathan away again the same way she had the day before.

'I want to finish my painting and do some things in the garden,' she told him firmly.

His quizzical look told her that he understood what she was doing but he agreed that he had work of his own to catch up on.

Late in the afternoon he came looking for her. Libby stood up as he walked through the hedge, her pulse thudding as she looked at him, powerfully male in tattered green shorts and running shoes. The long afternoons they'd spent swimming and walking and laughing together—balmy, sunny days of snatched pleasure that even now were beginning to seem like a dream—had lightly tanned his broad shoulders and bare muscled chest, and although her fingers ached with the need to touch him, to reassure herself that he was still with her, she clenched them by her side, his steady regard telling her it wasn't time for that now.

As if understanding her fears, Nathan contented himself with cutting the lawn with her ancient push-mower while Libby continued her weeding. The smell of freshly cut grass lingered in the air, and between the bursts of noise from the mower she could hear the high buzz of busy insects and the distant thudding of the sea beneath them. But for once the day's beauty left her unmoved.

Nathan finished the lawn and, leaving her to her weeds, disappeared into the kitchen, reappearing a short while later with a jug of lemonade. He sat beside her on the lawn and waited for her to remove her gloves, before passing her a glass of the chilled drink.

For a few minutes they sat quietly but then he sighed. 'What do you want me to do?' he asked finally, his voice edged with impatience. 'Just pack up and go without another word?'

She took a ragged breath, turning her head so that she looked out to sea. 'You said it all that day on the beach,' she said briskly, doing her best to sound efficient and sophisticated. 'There's nothing left to talk about. I'll have another glass, please.'

'Damn you, Libby.' Instead of pouring her one, he slammed his own glass back onto the tray, startling her so her eyes skidded back to meet his angry glare. 'I'm trying to manage some sort of apology here,' he grated.

Her stomach clenched. 'You don't owe me one.'

'That day on the beach I meant this to go one night,' he argued. 'But I didn't stop at one night.'

'I don't regret that.' She tilted her chin, keeping her gaze fiercely defiant. 'Do you?'

'What do you think?' he said, suddenly bleak, the anger seeming to drain from him.

Libby turned her head away again, looking out at the water, amazed that she was coping with this. 'I'm not as fragile as you think,' she said heavily. She turned back, meeting his steady gaze with a cool stare of her own. 'I do have a satisfying life here, Nathan,' she added brittly. 'I am going to miss you, of course, but one day there'll be other men.'

Instead of the relief she'd expected, his face closed like a mask and he said, 'You've changed.'

Not answering that, she leaned forward, her fingers tearing at a few sprigs of grass along the edge of the garden. 'Is Alistair home tomorrow?'

'Late, I should think,' he told her after a little while. 'He'll have flown into London this morning but he'll have people to see.'

'Will you wait to see him?'

'No.' Abruptly he stood. His hand came out and he drew her with him. 'I'm leaving early. Come and tell me what type of frame would be best,' he said, referring to the painting she'd given him so long ago. 'I need your advice.'

Later Libby made dinner but for once he seemed to have as little appetite as she. Leaving the food virtually untouched, they wandered out towards the cliff. A full moon irradiated the beach path with light and of one mind they walked down and stood, with hands entwined, on the sand.

The tide was at its highest and the sea rough, whitecaps glinting in the moonlight as the wind rose. It whipped her hair into a tangled net covering her face and suddenly she laughed, the solemnity of her mood crashing into recklessness. In one smooth movement she hauled her dress over her head.

Naked, she ran towards the churning water, calling for Nathan to follow as she dived eagerly into the cool waves.

He came after her, his face grimly set, seeming to share her urge to challenge the elements. They swam across the bay, fighting the drag of the tide, and she knew he must be aware of how dangerous it was but he seemed as beyond caring as she. As they returned he tried to catch her but she eluded him, diving swiftly between his thighs, laughing as he spun around searching for her.

Fiercely he swam towards her, catching her leg, but she was slippery and strong, fighting against him before sliding away, careless of her movements, not caring if she hurt him, wanting even to hurt him.

He grabbed for her again, then again, but each time she struggled, getting nearer and nearer the beach, until he shouted his frustration and she surged out of the water up towards the path, laughing at him, taunting him with her escape.

But he was fast, very fast, and her laughter turned to wild triumph at the set determination of him. He reached her within seconds, tackling her violently, moving over her as she tumbled on the beach, entering her roughly as she lay breathless and yearning.

He was untamed and she gasped at his power as he thrust her back into the sand. This was the way she'd wanted to see him, she rejoiced, abandoned, selfish, careless, his want so great it eclipsed his senses. Her nails scored the taut, muscled flesh of his shoulders as she lifted herself into him, fighting him, biting him, hating him, loving him. At the end he shouted her name, a fiercely possessive cry that rose against the wind and tipped her into delirious rapture.

Sunday morning dawned cool and misty, and when Libby finally hauled herself out of bed around seven her body ached with weariness. Even the cats seemed upset, mewing softly as they rubbed at her ankles, not touching the food she dished out for them. Sighing, she lifted them onto her knees, stroking their heads, wondering if Nathan would come and see her before he left for London.

After what had happened on the beach he'd seemed pre-occupied and distant, and she'd felt as if he'd withdrawn from her in everything but actual miles. He'd barely spoken on the way back up to the cliffs and then, instead of spending the night with her the way he had been since that first night, he'd muttered a vague excuse about needing to pack and returned to Alistair's cottage.

By eight she couldn't bear the waiting any longer but her legs were shaking as she ducked through the hedge and walked slowly towards the cottage. The cats scooted ahead, running in through the open kitchen door.

Nathan appeared, William in his arms, before she

reached the cottage. He didn't say anything, just watched her approach. 'I wanted to say goodbye,' she said stiltedly, forcing herself to meet his quiet blue-grey regard. 'Are you all packed?'

'Ready to leave.' He crouched and released her cat, tickling him under his ear and Duncan, too, as he nudged against him. 'You must tell me if anything happens,' he said, as he stood again. His face tightened as he registered her bewilderment. 'If you're pregnant,' he said flatly. 'After last night.'

Libby felt the colour drain from her face. The possibility hadn't even occurred to her, but as it did she felt her breath catch briefly before cold reason intervened. 'I won't be,' she said stiffly, folding her arms around her. 'It wasn't the right time.'

His expression didn't change but he handed her a sheet of paper which, she saw, bore a London telephone number. 'Nevertheless, these things happen. I'd want to know straight away.'

Despite knowing the chances of her being pregnant were non-existent, she folded the paper carefully and tucked it into the back pocket of her shorts. It was only a few numbers, but although she'd never dial them it felt like some sort of connection.

His eyes followed the movement and when he spoke his voice was raw, almost as if the words were being torn from him. 'Do you like children?'

She drew a sharp breath, feeling the cool air sharp in her lungs. 'Of course,' she said shakily. 'And one day I'd like my own. But I know my body, Nathan. There isn't a baby.'

'Call me regardless. So I know.'

She lowered her eyes. 'The traffic won't be bad at this hour. You should have quite a good run.'

He sent her a brief, unreadable look then bent to pet William again. He scooped him up, holding him so he stared into the cat's eyes. 'Look after your mistress.' He glanced down at Duncan. 'Both of you.' He lowered William and looked at Libby again. As if determined not to touch her, he slid his hands into the pockets of his jeans. 'If there's ever anything you need...'

'I'll call you,' she said quickly. 'Thanks.'

'I mean it, Libby.' Fractionally his voice hardened. 'I'd want to help.'

But she doubted his wife would be as eager. 'I won't come out to the car.' She held out her hand, praying he would not notice how it shook. 'Goodbye, Nathan.'

He took her hand, not shaking it but holding it firmly, his eyes darkening as he met hers. 'Goodbye, Libby. Look after yourself.'

'I will.' She dragged her hand away, breaking the last contact deliberately. 'Drive safely.' Then quickly, before she made a fool of herself, she gathered up the cats and walked speedily back to her cottage.

Shortly after, Libby heard his car start in the lane and she lifted her head from her bed where she'd flung herself. Gradually the sound of the engine grew softer as Nathan drove away until finally it had faded completely.

CHAPTER TEN

NATHAN'S registrar's eyebrows lifted when he greeted Nathan in his office on Monday morning. 'It was supposed to be a holiday,' Richard said easily. 'The tan's great but you look as tired as if you'd just spent a month on call.'

Nathan felt worse than if he had done. 'Any problems on the wards?'

'Not on the wards so much.' Richard took the coffee Nathan offered him and took the seat opposite. 'They've cut your Tuesday list,' he said flatly. 'Bloody cheek, waiting till you were away, but that's the current management for you.'

Nathan frowned. He'd spoken to the surgical manager the day before he'd left and had been told none of this. 'I'll speak with them today,' he said grimly. 'I can't run a decent service with just two half-day theatre sessions. They'll have to reverse the decision.'

Richard lifted his shoulders doubtfully. 'Things are tight,' he said bleakly. He took a mouthful of coffee and eyed Nathan over the top of the cup. 'This new chief executive officer who's taken over the trust comes straight from thirty years in big business. According to the press, he's never *been* in a hospital before let alone worked in one. He seems to think that by giving us a couple of day lists to play with we can churn through the numbers a bit and make the statistics look good and everyone will be happy.' He pushed the cup away, his face creased with disgust.

'Never mind the poor blokes who need their aneurysms and vessels done. Even the transplant beds have been cut.

135

Last week we had to send a donor kidney to London because we couldn't get ICU space. The beds were empty but
Administration wouldn't authorise the nursing staff.'

Briefly Nathan felt a shaft of longing for the peace of
Cornwall but he thrust the intrusive thought aside. 'This is
absurd,' he said wearily. 'This is a hospital, not a business.
Has the media been involved?'

Richard shook his head. 'Everyone's worried about their
jobs.'

'Perhaps we ought to worry more about our patients.'
Nathan drained his coffee, knowing he was no closer to
making a decision about his future plans than he had been
when he'd left, but perhaps this latest crisis would make
that decision for him. 'Let's see the wards before clinic.'

Because he'd been away, the only patients for him to see
were the ones who either Richard had operated on the week
previously or those who'd come in acutely over the last
few weeks, having previously been under his care.

One of those patients was a Mr McTaggart, a medically
frail but perky eighty-year-old man with chronic venous
ulceration of his lower legs. Nathan knew the man well.
Years ago one of the main arteries in his left leg had been
blocked by a clot, which had been flung off by his heart
during an arrhythmia, and Nathan had removed the embo-
lus and saved the leg. Subsequently, even though his leg
ulceration was unrelated to the original complaint, Nathan
continued to see him in his clinic and, knowing him so
well, had remained happy to do so.

Richard explained that he'd been admitted two weeks
previously with an infected ulcer, and although the infec-
tion had now cleared Nathan knew that trying to get it
healed was a task doomed to failure. In the past, out of
desperation, he'd resorted to grafting—with variable suc-
cess—but his patient's poor general health, his emphysema

and coronary heart disease meant an anaesthetic wasn't an agreeable thought.

'Mr Thomas!' The old man's face creased into a smile. 'I was hoping to see you this time. How are you doing?'

'Well, Mr McTaggart.' Nathan crouched by the bed, inspecting the ragged wound the charge nurse had carefully uncovered for him. It was basically clean now, and although the base looked relatively healthy there was no suggestion of healing. There were another two, smaller ulcers on his other leg, both clean but again not healing. He checked for pulses. 'How's your lovely wife?'

His patient chuckled. 'Och, she's all right,' he wheezed. 'Wee bit of angina but that's not so bad. She'll be pleased to hear you're back. Holiday, was it?'

'Something like that.' They chatted for a few more minutes and when they'd finished Richard stepped forward again.

'I see from the notes he's had everything in the past, including months of compression bandaging,' he said quietly. 'He's obviously not fit enough for an anaesthetic and even if he were I don't think we'd achieve anything. I thought we might just discharge him home to the care of the district nurse and GP and keep our fingers crossed.'

Nathan's eyes narrowed thoughtfully. Ignoring the way his gut clenched at his sudden memory of Libby, he turned to the ward pharmacist who'd joined his round and asked, 'What about some comfrey root? Can you make up a paste?'

She blinked. 'Comfrey, Mr Thomas? You mean…the plant?'

Out of the corner of his eye Nathan saw Richard choke. 'That's right,' he confirmed dryly. 'Worth a try, wouldn't you say?'

'Of course.' She still looked astonished. 'We do have a

herbal therapist attached to the department,' she said faintly. 'I'll see if he can organise something.'

'Good.' Nathan found himself rather enjoying his team's discomposure. 'Ask him to give me a call and we'll discuss it. He may have some other suggestions.' His mouth quirked. 'Marigold leaves and the like,' he muttered. He crouched down to explain to his patient. 'I think we'll try something herbal on these,' he said. 'Not exactly orthodox, but your ulcers have resisted everything else we've thrown at them.'

'Aye, I'll leave it up to you, Doctor. Anything to get me walking again.'

'Good man.' Nathan grinned. He nodded towards his house officer. 'Mary here will ask the physio and OT people to have a look at you and see if they can help with that as well, and then we'll let you home. It's difficult for you to get up to clinic so I'll drop by at the beginning of next week to see how you're getting on.'

'Very kind, Mr Thomas,' his patient said with a momentarily youthful beam. 'Very kind.'

Nathan grinned to himself as he noted his registrar's bemused expression. 'Come now, Richard,' he said sternly as they walked towards the next ward, 'comfrey's full of allantoin which, I'm sure you know, promotes new cell growth like almost nothing else on the market. Weren't you aware of that?'

'You're the boss,' Richard answered smoothly.

But the look Richard exchanged with both his house officers was doubtful to say the least, and Nathan laughed. He wasn't expecting any miracles from the comfrey but it seemed churlish not to try it when orthodox treatments had failed. 'Open your minds,' he teased.

'At least it'll be cheap.' The thought seemed to mollify some of Richard's doubt. 'I got an irate call from the surgical manager last week because we'd exceeded our drugs budget again last month.'

Nathan felt his good humour evaporate. Back to the real world, he thought grimly.

By late Friday afternoon he'd had enough. Not only was the administration determined to make the cut in his theatre time permanent, but it seemed they wanted one clinic session to go as well.

On top of everything else, at least four more ICU beds were to close, limiting the number of major procedures he could perform and meaning there'd be more of the dangerous transfers of seriously ill patients which seemed to be becoming the norm between London hospitals. In the four nights he'd been on call that week there'd already been two such transfers from St Stephen's and that was *before* any more closures.

His temper frayed by yet another fruitless clash—he and his fellow surgeons against the surgical manager—he stormed back to his office. Armed with his own and his colleagues' accounts of patients put at risk throughout the clinical fields, he dialled the number for the news desk of an evening newspaper.

After that things moved quickly. The journalist who visited him that night at home seemed surprised and concerned by his allegations. So far the cuts at St Stephen's had stayed out of the spotlight and the hospital had been used over the years by ministers on both sides as an example of the health reforms working. It seemed that the fact that budget cuts meant they were being forced to cut services to a minimum was going to be big news.

'The story will run Monday afternoon,' the journalist explained, after arranging to come in on Monday morning to take photographs. 'You might come in for a bit of publicity.'

But just how much publicity Nathan hadn't realised. The story of St Stephen's sinking standards, or TOP SURGEON SLAMS CUTS, as the paper chose to title it, triggered a massive amount of interest. It was taken up by all the major newspapers and television networks, and he acknowledged that he was probably fortunate he had no theatre list that Tuesday because he spent much of the day being interviewed and photographed by the news crews which set themselves up in the hospital foyer.

Paula called him on Tuesday night. He'd been interviewed in his office for television that evening and the process had taken so long that he'd had to stay late to finish his work. She caught him as he was finishing his dictation. 'You're behaving insanely, Nathan,' she said bluntly. 'They'll sack you.'

He leaned back in his chair, his eyes narrowing as he heard the fury she was trying so hard to conceal. 'Wouldn't you prefer that?' he asked coolly. 'Until now you've been keen enough on the idea of me leaving the NHS and joining you in private health care.'

'But you still need to retain some NHS commitment,' she countered. 'You'll seem so much more prestigious that way.'

He grimaced. 'You mean I'd attract more money.'

There was a brief pause. 'Of course that's not all I meant, darling,' she said, a little nervously now, as if she'd sensed his reaction to her words. 'I'm worried about your career. You're risking so much.'

Nathan sighed, realising he'd been unreasonable to expect her public support. Only two of his colleagues had backed his revelations in the media, although he suspected he had the private support of most of the rest of the hospital's clinical staff despite their refusals to comment. Nathan understood most people's reluctance to come forward into the spotlight for they'd be risking their own jobs, and in truth he barely understood his own recklessness. But he wasn't going to discuss that with Paula now. 'I'm tired,' he said finally. 'See you tomorrow in Theatre.'

He heard her say his name urgently but ignored it, letting the receiver drop back onto its cradle.

The telephone in his flat started ringing when he arrived home shortly before ten-thirty. His pulse thudded dully as he reached for it, but it was his mother on the other end.

'We saw you on the news tonight,' she said, once they'd exchanged greetings. 'We're very proud of you.'

He was touched by that. 'I might lose my job,' he warned.

'I'm sure you thought of that,' she said quietly, surprising him with her calmness. She hesitated. 'Nathan, I haven't mentioned it in months, and I know you've probably forgotten, but it's our thirtieth wedding anniversary on Saturday. We'd planned a little get-together for dinner at the house.'

Nathan frowned again, angry with himself for forgetting the occasion, but before he could say anything she rushed on. 'It's been so long and we'd love to see you…but, of course, we understand if you're working or on call—'

'I'll be there,' he interrupted firmly, acknowledging that her soft sound of surprise was not actually wholly unwarranted. But he had been intending to make more of an effort to spend time with the family. He refrained from asking whether Alistair was coming up from Cornwall for the evening, although it was the thing uppermost in his mind. 'What time?'

'Seven-thirty.' She sounded thrilled. 'And if there's someone you'd like to bring..? I mean, if you're seeing anyone at the moment…?'

He grimaced. 'I'll be coming alone,' he told her. 'Till Saturday, then.'

*   *   *

On Saturday morning he did a ward round with Richard, making sure there were no problems brewing for the weekend, especially since neither of them were on call. 'I expected to be doing this on my own,' Richard said, only half joking as they strode towards ICU. 'I thought you'd be looking for a new job by now.'

Nathan admitted he was just as surprised. The barrage of media reports at the beginning of the week had given way to a slow trickle, but he'd not heard a thing from the executive and hadn't even been asked to give an account of himself. He shrugged. 'Perhaps I'm too high-profile now,' he said ruefully, not sure if he was happy about that. 'I'm probably safe for life.'

Richard grinned. 'Don't bet on it,' he said lightly.

'The irony is, nothing's changed.' He pulled open the door to ICU, noting that although the unit was full there were two stripped beds in a side cubicle which had been labelled officially closed, with two or three more shortly to follow. 'They're maintaining the cuts.'

'It's not all been a lost cause.' Richard winked as they pulled on plastic aprons to cover their clothes and then washed their hands. 'It's early days and we all enjoyed seeing the CEO squirming on television.'

Their only patient there was a thirty-nine-year-old man with chronic renal failure caused by polycystic renal disease—an inherited condition which meant his kidneys had turned into great masses of cysts, wiping out virtually all the functioning tissue. The patient had been on haemodialysis for several years, but on Friday morning Nathan and Richard had transplanted a healthy kidney into the right side of his pelvis.

He was conscious now and weaned off his ventilator, and Nathan noted the urine output with approval. Clearly, the new kidney was working. The wound appeared healthy, there'd only been 150 ml drainage post-operatively, which was entirely satisfactory, and there were even a few bowel sounds present. 'You're doing well,' Nathan told him, smiling reassuringly. 'From a surgical point of view, everything's fine.'

'Thank you, Doctor.' The man's voice was still hoarse from the ET tube but he managed a weak smile. 'Do I stay here today?'

'Up to the medics,' Nathan explained, as the post operative care of post-transplant patients was shared between him and the renal physicians who took the major role. 'But you're doing so well I expect they'll take you back to the renal unit later on.'

The renal team joined them as they discussed the patient with two of the ICU doctors. Peter Jones, one of the renal consultants, said, 'I understand we've got you to thank, Nate, for being able to do this case at all. If it hadn't been for all the fuss this week, that bed would have closed on Wednesday and there wouldn't have been a spare bed for us yesterday.'

Nathan frowned, surprised, but the anaesthetist in charge of ICU confirmed Peter's words. 'That's right. Monday morning we were told to close another bed on Wednesday to go with the two which are supposed to close at the end of next week. Then on Tuesday afternoon everything changed.' He nodded to the closed cubicle by the door. 'There's even talk now of opening those two.' He grinned. 'We might almost be able to run a decent service again.'

'Only if we're allowed to operate again,' Nathan countered, but, still, he was buoyed by the news that he'd been wrong to assume that the publicity he'd provoked hadn't achieved anything concrete.

He'd intended to spend the rest of the weekend finishing the work he hadn't completed in Cornwall, but he couldn't muster any enthusiasm for it and instead he found himself later striding around his flat. It had been almost two weeks and Libby hadn't called. Did that mean she could be pregnant? Despite her avowals, he was familiar with the mechanical process of a woman's cycle and she should know for sure one way or the other quite soon.

Once then twice he reached for the phone, but he shoved it away each time. He'd give her another week, he vowed. One week and that was all. If she hadn't called he'd— He cut off the thought, frowning. The reality was that he didn't know what he'd do.

Opening the cupboard where he'd left the painting she'd given him, he lifted it out and for the umpteenth time that week unwrapped it. He studied the pale, sun-drenched landscape, his breath catching again at the memory of how she'd been...how untouched and soft she'd been that day.

His face hardened. Whatever innocence she'd still possessed at the end of his stay, he'd drained it with his fierceness the last night they'd spent together. It had been a selfish, thoughtless coupling, and it had destroyed whatever pretence he'd clung to about being in control of their affair. More than that even, he reflected solemnly, his absolute pleasure at the primitive embrace had shaken his understanding of his own nature.

His fingers clenched on the card but he forced himself to lessen his grip, knowing that however much pain it gave him he couldn't destroy it. It was a beautiful picture. It didn't deserve to spend its life shut away somewhere dark simply because he couldn't bear to have it on his walls. It felt like the most precious thing he owned, but he couldn't live with it.

Carefully he wrapped it again and strode to the door. Libby had told him what sort of frame he should buy and he knew his mother would love the picture. It would make a wonderful anniversary gift, trigger distant memories which he was sure remained precious to her. And at least that way it would be properly hung, without him being tortured by the different memories it evoked for him. His face set with determination. He was home now. Back at work and back in his real life. Libby didn't belong here.

It took longer than he'd expected to find the right frame and get it fitted, and the traffic was bad so it was almost seven by the time he returned. He took a brief shower and dressed quickly, before leaving for his mother's home in Surrey.

The long, sweeping driveway leading up to the graceful Georgian house was crowded with cars, and he grimaced as he parked the Saab on the road outside, realising this wasn't exactly going to be the quiet occasion she'd led him to expect. Clearly the family had turned out *en masse*.

It was a warm evening, still very light, and all the front windows of the house and the doors had been flung open. As he approached the door the crunch of his steps on the gravel was drowned by music, laughter and the echoing sound of children's feet on the stairs which seemed to fly out into the soft spring air.

Unaccountably the hairs on the back of his arms rose, and for one second he froze at the door, just one second, but it was long enough for his eyes to fix on the slender figure of a woman barely visible behind the net curtains of the kitchen window.

Suddenly his mother was welcoming him and it was too late to back away and he found himself drawn inside, inevitably, to Libby.

CHAPTER ELEVEN

ALISTAIR had scolded her for staying in the kitchen but Libby was content, helping his mother. The sheer numbers and boisterous noisiness of his family—even without the one member she knew could affect her like no other—overwhelmed her, and so she lingered there, tearing basil leaves for a salad. She heard Alistair's mother's voice behind her, heard several voices, wiped her hands on her apron, turned round and felt her world rock.

She clutched the edge of the bench for support, but everybody was spilling into the room and they were laughing and talking and shouting all at once and unwrapping parcels. She saw his pallor as he came towards her, and it was as if Nathan and she were alone in this place of madness.

'I—I didn't know,' she managed, her voice raw and torn like the basil. 'Alistair said you wouldn't come.'

'It's all right.' His voice was as strained as hers, and she knew that nothing was all right. Nothing.

And then his mother was beside him. 'Nathan, it's beautiful,' she was saying, and it was Libby's painting she was showing everyone. 'I adore it. Thank you.'

Libby felt Nathan's gaze searing across her face but she turned back to the sink, her fingers going automatically to the tray of tomatoes on the bench. Carefully she lifted one, turned on the tap, rinsed the tomato, then placed it in a colander to drain. Then she took another. On her fourth, or perhaps her fifth, Alistair stopped her.

'Leave them, Libby,' he was saying, his arm urging her away. 'Everybody's here now. Come and let me introduce you. Come and have some fun.'

She wouldn't have 'fun' but Libby let him turn her around. Nathan was still in the kitchen, by the door now, a beer in his hand, talking with the kindly man she knew was his stepfather. They both dropped their eyes to Alistair's hand at her waist. The older man's face creased with mild interest but for a fraction of second before he masked it Libby saw Nathan's fury.

She paled, brushing Alistair's friendly arm away and managing a quick smile when he blinked at her in obvious puzzlement. He looked swiftly towards Nathan and then brightened, as if he understood her concern. 'You two know each other, don't you?' He grinned at her. 'Presumably you met or did Nathan do his "my work is my life" bit and lock himself away with his computer all month?'

'W-we've met.' Libby forced her mouth into a smile but it felt stiff and uncomfortable.

Nathan lifted his beer, taking several mouthfuls and saying nothing, but the tension in the room must have been obvious enough for even Alistair to sense it because his laugh was a little strained. 'I should have warned you,' he said to Libby. He looked at his father, explaining, 'Libby's a herbal therapist.'

'Ah, I see.' The older man's eyes twinkled at Nathan. 'So you argued?' When there was no immediate reply from his stepson he smiled kindly at Libby. 'I wouldn't worry, my dear. It's not meant personally. Nathan's more conservative than the rest of us. He's probably a bit intolerant of alternative medicine.'

Startled, her eyes flew to Nathan's set face. 'But he isn't—'

'Leave it, Libby.' Cool blue-grey eyes slammed into her widened green ones. 'Not now.'

She frowned, not understanding, but then his mother swirled into the room, and there were other people and more noise and people were shaking Nathan's hand and congratulating him about something, but before she could make sense of it Alistair was tugging her away and they were moving towards the room across the hall.

Dinner was a noisy, chaotic buffet, and there were so many people—so many brothers and sisters of Alistair, and uncles and aunts, and, it seemed, dozens and dozens of children, all spilling around the table and flooding through the house—that Libby felt as if this must be the biggest family in the world.

'Only eight,' Nathan told her neutrally, when she questioned him faintly after finding herself somehow beside him in the confusion of the crowd. 'There are only eight of us children but Alistair and I are the only unmarried ones and the rest have bred like rabbits.'

He looked down at her and she knew that while, for the benefit of the others, his expression suggested he was amused by her bemusement, underneath that there lurked something far more disturbing. 'It's not so many.'

'It is if you're an only child of parents who were only children.' She jostled her plate as a couple of identical toddlers clutched at her legs on their way across the room.

'These are Matthew and Jason. Lucy's twins.' Grinning suddenly, Nathan dumped his plate and scooped up the nearest of the pair with a casual ease that suggested genuine enjoyment of the children's company. 'Say hello, Jason.'

The child beamed at her, hiccuping slightly as Nathan shoved him into Libby's arms, forcing her to deposit her barely touched meal back onto the table. She smiled and bounced the child on her hip. He was like a little cherub, cute with bright red cheeks and masses of blond curls.

Nathan picked up the child's twin and looked at him doubtfully. 'Oh, no, I think this might be Jason,' he said hesitantly. 'Or is it?' He shook the giggling toddler gently, tipped him upside down, as if looking for a label, then held him at arm's length as his short legs pedalled furiously in the air. 'Name, child? Name?'

Libby laughed and the child she was holding promptly stuck his fingers into her mouth, his other hand tugging at her hair, pulling half of it loose from her carefully arranged topknot, gurgling his delight as her hair tumbled across his face.

Nathan's face seemed to still. He returned the child he was holding to the floor, then held out his arms for hers, his eyes unreadable as they surveyed the damage his nephew had wrought. 'Sorry,' he said quietly. He lifted a hand to slowly tuck her hair away behind her ear and the gentle caress turned her legs weak. 'I'll take him while you fix it.'

She passed the child across, flinching from the heat that sparked where their hands met briefly, but she dared not look up. She turned away abruptly, busying her hands with her hair. Then she saw that Alistair was watching them, his brow furrowed as his regard shifted to Nathan.

Libby let her hair drop, her mouth drying in alarm. She swung back to Nathan, but he'd seen Alistair now, too, and he was returning his stare with a bland coldness that bore no trace of brotherly love.

Libby shivered. She had to do something, she realised, sudden fear that the men would fight making it difficult to think straight. She couldn't bear to be responsible for a rift between the brothers. Muttering something vague about needing a mirror for her hair she walked quickly towards the door.

Upstairs, thankfully, it was quiet, and she walked along the broad passageway to the bedroom Alistair's mother had shown her to earlier. It had once been Alistair's twin sisters' room, and although the subdued pastel wallpaper and furnishings looked relatively recent, the shelves lining the walls were still crammed with books about horses and photographs of the girls, riding, hung above the beds.

Pale twilight filtered in through the small end window and she didn't bother turning on the lamp. Leaving the door slightly ajar, she perched nervously on the end of one of the beds. While she waited she released the rest of her hair and combed nervous fingers through it to restore some sort of order.

Nathan wasn't long. She'd known he wouldn't be. He shut the door behind him and leaned back against it, watching her. 'Since there's no one to hear us now,' he said quietly, 'suppose you tell me what's going on.'

'I was coming up for a course,' she said huskily. 'It's been arranged for months. It's a five-day seminar that one of the universities is offering. Alistair was driving up anyway. He bullied and bullied me. In the end it seemed the simplest thing to come with him and then he insisted I stay here but I should never—'

'I don't mean why you're here,' he interrupted. 'I mean, what's going on between you and my brother? If there's nothing between you, why is he looking at me like that?'

She shuddered, remembering the way he'd returned Alistair's look. 'Nothing! There is nothing between us. We're neighbours and friends. Nothing has changed.'

'Has he touched you?'

'No! Nathan—'

'He's brought you to meet his family.'

'It doesn't mean anything.' She lowered her head to her hands, hiding her face from him. 'Stop it.'

'But he's kissed you.'

She froze, remembering the fumbled embrace which had embarrassed her this morning, embarrassed her and worried her until she'd explained it away by deciding to consider it part of Alistair's naturally exuberant friendship. 'No, not the way you're thinking. He hasn't kissed me.'

'Sure, Libby?'

His voice was very low now and she lifted her head, glad of the partial darkness as it would conceal her flush. 'Yes.'

'Liar.' He was by her in moments, lifting her from the bed. 'Kenneth saw you,' he told her softly, referring to his stepfather by name. 'He saw you together in the garden. You were in his arms.' His grip on her arms tightened. 'My parents think he's about to propose. The whole family is talking about it.'

'They can't be.' She swayed, dizzy, would have fallen if not for his support. 'It's not true,' she said hoarsely. 'All right, he kissed me, yes, but it wasn't—'

But he hauled her against him and his mouth covered hers and drowned the words. It was a brief, fiery kiss, hard and passionate, and when he lifted his head she was shaking. Unconsciously she murmured an appeal, tilting her head up, but he pulled sharply back.

'Did you do that with him?' he murmured thickly. 'Beg for more?'

'No!'

His big hand slid up, cupping her bare breast beneath the amber linen of her dress. 'What about this?' he muttered, his eyes narrowing at her gasp as he brushed her tautening nipple. 'Did this swell for my brother?'

She closed her eyes, her breath quickening. 'He's never touched me,' she whispered desperately.

'He wants to.' Roughly Nathan tipped her back onto the bed, following her, edging her thighs apart so he lay between them, his head level with hers. 'You're such a sensualist,' he whispered, mocking the wantonness that arched her body against him. 'Is this how you'll open yourself to him?'

'No!' But the word came out as a groan, a long, sensual moan as his mouth dropped to the breast his busy fingers had now freed. Downstairs, beneath this room, she could hear the muffled noise of his family—voices, laughter, the scraping of plates—but nothing mattered except Nathan and what he was doing to her.

Dimly she was aware of urgent, determined hands removing her dress, her briefs and finally her stockings. 'Nice,' he murmured, his mouth tracing the faint line where they'd gripped the tops of her thighs. Briefly he bit into her taut flesh, lifting his head at her soft cry. 'Did you buy them, thinking of Alistair?'

She shook her head numbly. Her hands fluttered to the front of the white shirt he wore beneath his dark suit, but he pushed them away impatiently, his eyes dropping to her thighs, his body sliding down the bed. 'Say my name,' he demanded, his mouth going lower.

'Nathan,' she whispered, catching her breath. 'Nathan. Nathan…Nathan…'

'Louder.'

She buried her hands in his hair, clenching her fists. 'Nathan,' she gasped, feeling the urgency building, not caring that if anybody was outside the door they'd hear her, not caring if the world ended. She loved him and he was with her and that and this were everything. 'Nathan. Nathan…'

But afterwards, instead of making love with her as she craved he evaded her seeking hands, lifting himself away from her damp body so she cried in pain, his rejection scoring her like a rake.

When he sat beside her, close but not touching, she snatched up her dress, suddenly self-conscious, covering her cooling body, hating the way something which seconds ago had been so heated and promising now just seemed sordid and futile. She was like a hungry bird, she thought helplessly, desperately snatching whatever crumbs he chose to throw her.

After several long minutes he rested his hand on her bare hip, his touch without passion but gentle and soothing, as if he sensed her desolation. 'That last night,' he said coolly. 'Are you pregnant?'

She shivered. 'No.'

'You didn't call me.'

She didn't say anything, and after another few minutes of heavy silence he lifted his hand. 'I don't want Alistair near you,' he said quietly. 'I have no right to ask anything of you but still I am asking for that.'

She curled herself tighter. To so hate the idea of her being with Alistair he must be convinced she'd tell him about their affair, and that the news would reach his Paula. 'I don't want Alistair to touch me,' she said huskily, driven to reassure him if only to lessen his fears. 'There's nothing between us.'

'You've said that before.'

Didn't he understand she'd never willingly hurt him, never reveal what had happened to anyone, never come between him and his brother? 'He's just a friend,' she whispered.

'He thinks he's in love with you. You'll have to tell him straight.'

Before Alistair's embrace this morning in the garden she would have argued with him, but now, hesitantly, she allowed space for doubt. 'I will.'

'Before I leave. Tonight.'

'No. Not tonight.' She couldn't do anything like that tonight, not the way she was now. 'Tomorrow,' she said hoarsely, struggling into a sitting position because that might give her a little dignity. She hugged the dress to her breasts, hiding herself. 'I'll tell him tomorrow.'

His mouth twisted and she wondered if it was her gesture or her words that were responsible. 'Tomorrow,' he agreed finally. Abruptly the bed dipped as he levered himself up.

He strode to the door, opened it then hesitated. In the late evening light his face was shadowed, but from the stiff way he stood she sensed he felt uncomfortable about leaving like this, although, she thought miserably, that was nothing compared with the way she felt, watching him go.

'Thank you,' he said finally, his voice very low and rough-edged so it rasped across her nerves. 'I'll never ask you for anything else.'

The next morning she rose early and dressed. Not wanting to disturb Alistair or his parents, she tiptoed downstairs. The living rooms and kitchen had been left untidy after the party, and plates and glasses and discarded party hats and streamers littered the floor and tables. Needing something to keep herself occupied, she located a supply of plastic rubbish sacks and began sorting through the mess.

She was stacking the last of an enormous pile of dishes into the dishwasher when her hostess appeared in the kitchen. 'Oh, Libby, thank you, but you shouldn't have,' she exclaimed, gazing around the newly straightened room in dismay. 'You're our guest.'

'And it was *your* celebration,' Libby countered lightly, filling the sink with hot water to wash the crystal by hand. 'You shouldn't have to do the cleaning up.'

'I'm used to it,' she said with a wry smile. 'When you've brought up as many children as I have you learn all about cleaning up.' She switched on the kettle. 'I desperately need a cup of tea. You too?'

'Please.' Libby pulled on a pair of yellow rubber gloves and began washing the glasses. 'I'm sorry I left so early last night,' she said hesitantly. 'It was a long drive up and I was very tired.'

Briefly Libby found herself surveyed by shrewd, warm, brown eyes. 'Nathan mentioned you had a headache. Are you better now?'

Libby flushed. 'Much,' she said stiffly, lowering her head hastily back to the dishes. 'Thank you.'

The older woman poured the boiling water into a teapot and assembled a tray. 'Leave those,' she said firmly, nodding to the rest of the glasses. 'It's such a lovely morning—let's take our drinks outside. Alistair tells me you're a keen gardener and I need your advice on mine.'

However, her garden—a beautifully landscaped collection of mature willow at the river, coming back to oaks, camellias, then roses and summer flowers, all balanced by the riotous collection of late-flowering bulbs which flooded the front lawn—was superb, and clearly she had no need of Libby's advice.

Instead, as they strolled around the property, it seemed she wanted to talk about her children and mainly, to Libby's dismay, about Alistair and Nathan. After a few general comments she asked, 'Did you notice how different from the others Nathan is?'

Libby frowned. 'Well, the rest are fair,' she admitted. 'Like you and Kenneth.'

'Nathan takes after his father,' she was told. His mother explained that her first husband had died when Nathan was a child, something Libby already knew from Alistair, although she didn't stop the older woman.

'I'd only left them for an hour,' the older woman said softly. 'He had a heart attack. Very sudden, quite out of the blue. By the time I got home the ambulance was taking him away, but it was too late, of course.'

She blinked several times and Libby touched her arm. 'We don't have to talk about this.'

'No, I want to.' The older woman gave her a quick, almost nervous smile. 'Nathan was a serious little boy. In the hour I was away that afternoon he matured ten years. I was hysterical, screaming, crying, but he was very calm.

He'd called the ambulance himself,' she said ponderously, tilting her head. 'He was barely seven.'

Libby could visualise him doing that. Even if she hadn't seen him dealing so calmly with Dorothy Penrose that afternoon, she wouldn't have been able to imagine him not coping with anything.

'He's never talked about that day,' his mother said huskily, as they paused to enjoy the scent of some tiny blue hyacinths, 'but when he decided to do medicine I knew why.'

They walked on, Libby wondering tensely where this was all leading, and then his mother said quickly, 'I remarried very quickly. Within six months. Kenneth was a friend of my husband's. He'd been widowed with two very young children and marriage seemed to make sense for both of us.' She smiled at Libby's dismayed expression.

'Oh, I loved him in my own way,' she said quietly. 'And later we had Peter and Lucy and then Alistair and the twins, and that love grew into the precious thing we have now.'

'How did Nathan feel about his new family?' Libby asked hesitantly, aching for the child he had been.

They'd reached a small rose garden now. The flowers were budding and she could see that in a few weeks they'd be glorious. They sat on the wooden bench in the middle and her hostess sighed. 'He was very good with them,' she replied. 'Kenneth's children adored Nathan from the start, and it must be obvious to you from seeing them last night that the others still worship him as well.

'But even when he was a child himself, he took his role as the oldest very seriously. He always looked out for them, was always there when they needed him, even though there must have been times when he longed to be left alone with his friends or his studies. On the surface Nathan always seems relaxed and at ease, but beneath that, Libby, beneath that, he takes his responsibilities to heart.'

She twisted her hands together. 'We don't see so much of him now that they're all grown-up. He works too hard,' she said, clenching her fists to emphasise the words. 'I worry about him.' Her mouth twisted ruefully, a gesture Libby recognised from Nathan. 'He's very like his father.'

Libby swallowed, fixing her gaze rigidly on the roses. 'You're worried about him having a heart attack like his father?'

'Nathan's far heaithier,' his mother said firmly, and Libby looked up in time to catch her shaking her head confidently. 'His father had a stressful job, yes, but he was also unfit and overweight and he was a heavy smoker. Nathan's always been very fit. He runs and he plays squash and he's never smoked. No, I'm more worried about his emotional health. I'd like to see him happy, Libby. He deserves that. I'd like to see him really happy.'

Libby's breath had escaped in a long puff of relief at his mother's reassurance about Nathan's risk of heart disease, but at her next words she stiffened.

'Of all the children, I think Alistair's closest to him,' the other woman said carefully. 'Which, my dear, is where we both know you come in.'

Libby's pulse thudded. 'W-what are you saying?'

'They both have feelings for you.'

'No!' She sat up very straight, her back like a rod against the bench. 'You're wrong.'

'Alistair's like a butterfly,' she continued, ignoring Libby's faint denial. 'He's still young. He flits from job to job, woman to woman, happy just to sample life at the moment. But I know him, Libby. I've watched him with you. If you give him the right encouragement he'll settle.'

Libby couldn't stop herself asking, 'And Nathan?'

'Nathan's far more complex.'

Libby moistened her parched lips. 'He doesn't want me,'

she said huskily. 'Alistair…might have feelings for me but I don't return them.'

'I don't mean to embarrass you by interfering, Libby.' The older woman hesitated a few seconds. 'But did you see Nathan on television last week?'

Libby looked up sharply. 'Television?'

'He was speaking out against the reforms at St Stephen's. He was very good, very…angry.' She leaned forward, her hands clasped on her knees.

'I was stunned. In the past I'm sure he would have stood back. He'd have worried more about what might happen to his patients if he lost his job. He would have fought from within the system, not opposed it so publicly.' She stared into the distance. 'He's changed somehow. I knew for sure when he gave me your painting.'

Libby flushed, knowing what painting she meant, and her hostess's eyes blinked an acknowledgement of her comprehension. 'Alistair told me it looked like one of yours,' she said quietly. 'And I knew it was Cornwall. You can tell by the coastline and the light.'

'Is that significant?'

'Before Nathan's father died we spent our last summer holidays together by the sea in Cornwall,' she said huskily. 'It was a wonderful, happy time, just the three of us.' She dabbed her eyes with the corner of her handkerchief. 'Nathan's very perceptive. He would have known the painting would remind me.'

She sniffed, smiling her gratitude for the comforting hand Libby rested on her arm. 'The old Nathan wouldn't have wanted to cause me pain by that. He'd have wanted to protect me. He'd have thought that the best thing for me would be to forget my time with his father and live life in the present. But last night he seemed… I think he's become more emotional. More open to his feelings. Less coolly clinical. I think you were the catalyst for that change.'

'He doesn't love me,' Libby said thickly. 'He's...' But if Nathan hadn't told his family about Paula yet it wasn't her place to. 'He's seeing someone else. I've met her. She's very beautiful.'

His mother shook her head. 'Libby, I heard you together last night.' She lowered her eyes at Libby's shocked gasp. 'I was looking for Nathan, you see. I saw him go upstairs and when he didn't come down I was worried. He gets such terrible migraines—'

'I know,' Libby whispered fiercely, remembering what had happened the night before and unable to look at her. 'But it wasn't what you think—'

'I know my son,' she interrupted. 'If he was committed to another woman, he'd never have gone near you. Not...not unless he was so in love with you that that over-whelmed his conscience.'

His mother didn't understand and Libby could hardly explain that he'd only touched her in the first place at Paula's urging, because even for her that was still a shock-ing thing to contemplate. She stood. 'I can't talk about this,' she said abruptly. 'I'm sorry.'

But Nathan's mother was persistent, and although Libby tried to avoid any more tête-à-têtes she was staying in her home and it wasn't always easy to escape them.

By Friday afternoon, after the end of her course, the day before Alistair was to drive her back to Cornwall, knowing she might never see Nathan again, her determination to stay away from him crumbled.

She longed to believe his mother, ached to believe that she'd been right about him not truly loving Paula. And no matter how the sane part of her urged her to flee from more rejection, she'd never told him how much she loved him, not properly—only that one time and then he hadn't be-lieved her and she hadn't tried to persuade him. She couldn't live the rest of her life wondering if things might have been different if she had.

CHAPTER TWELVE

NATHAN grinned his approval at the fit-looking man he'd just examined in his clinic that afternoon. 'Well done,' he said, congratulating him on winning a local bowls tournament. 'Hard to believe it's less than two months since I did that.' He ran his finger along the lengthy incision down the centre of his patient's abdomen, now well healed. 'But weren't you advised to take it easy for a while?'

'Oh, easy!' The man flapped his hand dismissively as he sat up. 'Two months ago I'd have won the regional title,' he said flatly. 'Going for the local's easy enough.'

Nathan's mouth twitched as he folded away the Doppler machine he'd used to assess the blood flow in his patient's feet. 'This must be some sort of record. A ruptured aneurysm's about as major a crisis as there is. Not many people would be happy on the bowling green yet, if ever.'

While he waited for his patient to dress he flipped through the notes in his office. He'd performed the emergency operation the night before he'd left for Cornwall. He stilled momentarily. Cornwall. Just the name now evoked abrupt longing in him.

But he would get over that. His expression hardened and he forced his attention back to his work. He saw that Richard had discharged his patient only eight days after the operation, so his post-op progress had obviously been excellent. Carefully he checked all the blood and X-ray results, making sure nothing had been missed.

He looked up as the man walked easily back into the room. 'I see your blood cholesterol was high when you

160

were in,' he said. 'That's a risk factor for hardening of the arteries. Has anybody talked to you about that?'

'That young chap…Mr Price. Richard, was it?' At Nathan's nod he continued, 'He's arranged for me to see a heart doctor next week. They told me to wear comfortable clothes and shoes because they might want to put me on one of those exercise machines. Meantime, he's had a word with my GP who's given the wife a diet for me and told me to have a glass or two of red wine instead of the beer.' He sniffed. 'Not so easy,' he said gruffly. 'But if it helps my bowls I'll cope.'

'Good.' He shook the man's hand. 'Ask Reception for an appointment to see me in six months,' he told him. 'If there's any reason to see me earlier, either you or your GP should contact my secretary to arrange it, but I don't foresee any problems.'

'Right you are, Doctor.'

Nathan closed the door behind the man with a wry grin. His patients invariably held surprises for him. Seeing someone who'd been critically ill now enjoying life to the fullest, that was enormously rewarding. It was a reminder of the good he could do and, considering how near he'd been to leaving lately, it was a reminder he needed.

The clinic sister bustled in and deposited another heap of notes on his desk. 'Running early for once,' she said brightly. 'Your last three new patients of the afternoon are here. Two with varicose veins, cubicles one and two, and a man with severe claudication, cubicle five.' She slapped one set of notes onto the side bench. 'Plus one DNA,' she added, the initials standing for 'did not arrive'. 'He's an eighty-year-old with a query aneurysm but there's no record of a scan. I'll give his GP a ring and see if we can organise him for Monday's clinic. All right?'

'Fine.' Nathan picked up the first set of notes and read

the referral letter her GP had sent, but just as he was about to go and see the patient the phone shrilled.

It was his secretary at the other end. 'There's a Libby Deane here to see you,' she explained. 'I've explained you're very busy but she's insisting on waiting.'

He sat on the edge of the desk, and after a few seconds Mrs Langley said sharply, 'Mr Thomas? Are you still there?'

Nathan frowned. 'Ask Libby to wait in my office,' he said carefully. 'You'd better warn her I might be a while.' He replaced the receiver and leaned back in his chair, his eyes closed, acknowledging and dismayed by the sudden pounding of his pulse.

After he'd seen his last patient Richard wanted his advice on some of the cases he'd seen, and then his registrar had some questions about the following week's lists. By the time Nathan was finally striding back towards his office he realised that Libby had been waiting over an hour.

His fists clenched on the notes he was carrying as he tried to prepare himself for this meeting. Compared with the established routine of his daily life and his work at St Stephen's, his few weeks with Libby in Cornwall had been idyllic. But they'd passed and that had been for the best and he had to stop thinking about her.

She was a beautiful, free spirit, enticing and intriguing, but she wasn't for him and he'd only hurt her by leaving her with any hope that there could be a future for them. One day she'd meet someone who would live with her there in Cornwall, and she'd bear beautiful children who'd lead free, serene lives by the beach, and everything would be perfect for her.

And him? Nathan's mouth tightened. He'd be here, in London, working as he always worked, and happy in his own way. Paula was still making it clear she wanted to marry him, and since she'd now decided she could have a child, if that was what he wanted, the most sensible thing would be for him to agree to that and be grateful he'd found a woman who would understand the demands of his career and who wouldn't create any upheaval in his life.

Eventually he'd remember his time with Libby as merely a pleasant interlude in an otherwise unremarkable life.

Libby jumped up when he entered and, startled by the primitive urge to wrench her glorious hair loose of its confining clasp, his voice was perhaps harsher than it ought to have been as he demanded, 'What's happened? Why are you here?'

Pink colour rushed into her cheeks but her beautiful eyes didn't flinch and she tilted her brave little chin up to him, although the hands that plucked anxiously at the pale fabric of her dress belied her transparent attempts to appear calm. 'Nothing's happened.' The soft huskiness of her voice reminded him uncomfortably of the way she'd cried his name on Saturday. 'I wouldn't have come here only I didn't know how else to find you.' She bit softly on her lower lip and he felt his thighs tauten as he followed the familiar nervous gesture. 'I wanted to talk.'

'How did Alistair take it?' he asked abruptly, forcing himself to think of anything but reaching for her and wrenching her into his arms.

Her brow creased. 'He didn't seem unduly upset.' Her eyes dropped before he could read her expression. 'I suspect you overestimated his feelings for me.'

Nathan doubted that but he refrained from commenting. He was still shaken by the fury that had flooded him at the sight of the two of them together, and the irony that his viewpoint had switched completely since he'd made love with Libby—from wanting to stay away from her for his brother's sake to now wanting almost to kill Alistair for touching her—was not lost on him.

He knew that if she hadn't agreed to discourage Alistair

on Saturday it would have been a struggle to keep his hands from his brother's neck and, given that he'd never wanted to harm another human being in his life, the violent emotion he'd experienced still frightened him. He took a deep, wrenching, calming breath. 'When are you going home?'

'Tomorrow.' She sat again, her movements uncharacteristically awkward, the way she crossed her legs giving him a disturbing glimpse of slender calf before she straightened her dress. 'Nathan, your mother's been talking to me.'

He folded his arms, feeling his expression hardening. 'And?'

'She knows about us.' She was keeping her eyes on the hands she held clasped in her lap. 'She...' her colour deepened hotly '...heard us. Upstairs. On Saturday.'

Nathan had wondered about that. He'd seen her curiosity when he'd come downstairs to say his farewells. 'So what?' he said flatly. 'Tell her to mind her own business.'

But Libby seemed flustered by that. Her hands brushing her dress over her slender hips, she jumped up again and walked to the window, looking out, facing away from him, silent again.

'Libby, I don't care if my mother...disapproves. I certainly can't see why it should matter to you.'

'She doesn't disapprove,' she said faintly

He blinked. 'What?'

'Actually, she seemed to approve.' Slowly, very slowly, she turned around, and although he could see every inch of her exquisite shape silhouetted against the light her face was shadowed. 'She seems to think I can make you happy. You see, I told her I loved you.'

Nathan closed his eyes briefly. 'Now tell me,' he said finally, 'that you didn't mean that.'

She didn't move, but he saw her fingers whiten with the pressure of gripping the window ledge behind her. 'But I do love you.' Each word drove into him like a separate, thorny spike. 'I tried to tell you properly the night you told me Paula was coming, but you wouldn't be persuaded.'

'Libby…?' He wanted to go to her, make her see sense, but, knowing the folly of touching her, he stayed by his desk. It was important to restore some sanity to his life. 'I *can't* love you,' he said grimly, wincing as she flinched from his uncompromising honesty.

'My life is here with my work and your life will always be in Cornwall. I can't give you what you want. I'm not right for you. Being with me would destroy everything that makes your life so right for you. There is no future for us. You're a romantic, I know that, but one day you'll understand and then you'll be grateful that I'm not. I'm sorry, Libby. Terribly sorry.'

She spun back towards the window. 'But you wanted me.'

'Of course I wanted you. You've the body of an angel.'

'And Saturday?'

He lowered his head. When the reality of her had intruded into his real world, as had happened on Saturday, he acknowledged, it was more difficult to rationalise away his passion. For he hadn't been sensible then. There had been no doubt of his emotions that night. His mouth tightened. His desire to hit out at Alistair, passionate and almost uncontrollable, had been exceeded only by his need to touch her himself, to make her cry out the need for him he knew his experience could induce. 'I gave you pleasure, didn't I?' he said painfully. 'Wasn't that what you wanted?'

'No!' The cry was anguished. 'Not pleasure, like that, on its own. I wanted you to make love to me.'

'There's no point to this, Libby.' He'd been out of control on Saturday and he didn't want to feel that way again. He'd intended to make love to her so wildly his fever would have left traces upon her body. Then, like some sort of primitive savage enforcing his territorial rights, he'd half planned to drag her downstairs and display her to Alistair and the rest of his family to prove to them that she was his.

If she had fought him he'd have been driven to it, he realised. But her submission had been his salvation, had brought him to his senses and had given him the strength to draw away before he'd destroyed everything. He forced his mind back to what they were discussing now, deliberately voicing his determination. 'I'll never touch you again.'

He saw her draw herself up stiffly. 'I knew all that,' she said quietly, as if she were speaking to herself. 'You told me on the beach that day it was only sex for you. I knew that.'

He ached for her but he had no choice. 'Libby, it's for the best. Later, you'll understand that and agree with me.'

She turned around. With exaggerated carefulness, not looking at him again, she retrieved a small, dark bag from beside the chair and approached the door. 'Goodbye, Nathan.' Her voice was small and formal. 'Sorry to have disturbed your work. I understand how important it is to you. I won't bother you again.'

He stood up abruptly, alarmed by her brittle pallor. 'Where are you going now?'

'Home. I've changed my mind about staying another night. I'll get the next train from Paddington. Alistair can bring my things when he drives down tomorrow.'

He reached for his keys, suddenly unwilling to let her go alone. 'I'll drive you to the station.'

'I'm not about to throw myself under a train,' she said carefully.

Nathan winced. 'Don't, Libby.'

He opened the door and she walked out into Mrs Langley's office, although thankfully his secretary had already left. 'I'm not going anywhere with you, Nathan.' Her words were crisply determined but he could hear the shake in her voice. 'So there's really no point in following me. Please, don't try and bully me. I want to go alone.

'Oh, and there's something I should have mentioned on Saturday night.' She turned around, her expression very controlled. 'Dorothy Penrose is doing very well. It turns out that three of the blood vessels supplying her heart were badly blocked and that was the reason for her angina and heart attack. She's had bypass surgery now and she's expecting to be allowed home any day.'

'Thank you.' Nathan had been in touch with the hospital himself regularly and was aware of Dorothy's progress, but he didn't explain. He just stayed there, in the doorway of his secretary's office, his heart pounding, telling himself he'd done the right thing as Libby turned away from him again and walked along the hospital corridor and out of his life.

'New Zealand!' Alistair's eyebrows soared. 'You're mad! Why, Libby? Why? You belong here. In Cornwall.'

Carefully Libby poured the mixture of steeped sage leaves, alcohol and water into the muslin bag she'd fitted into the wine press she used for making tinctures. 'One of my father's cousins lives out there,' she said quietly. 'I've written to her since I was a child. It's time I visited.'

'So visit her,' he spluttered. 'You don't need to emigrate!'

'I'm not emigrating.' She sent him a vague, distracted smile, concentrating on pressing the dark liquid into a jug. 'I'm only going for six months at first. Just as a tourist.'

He was pacing her workroom, but at her words he swivelled back to her. 'But if you like it you'll stay?'

'Possibly. Assuming I can get immigration clearance. The man at the embassy told me that it should be possible if I'm prepared to invest enough money in the country.'

'When? When are you going?'

'Two weeks on Monday.' She frowned slightly, forcing the pump lower to drain the rest of the juice. 'From Heathrow.'

'What about the cats?' He gestured to where William and Duncan watched them from the hall. At her surprised look he scowled, reminding her of a young child not getting his own way. 'Are they going?'

She strained the liquid into two small labelled jars. 'Of course.'

'You're putting them through quarantine? Letting them be locked in a tiny cage for months?'

She winced at her animals' stares, suddenly accusing as if they'd understood Alistair's words. 'I don't want to,' she admitted, 'but there's no choice.' She stared pointedly back into William's cross face. 'I can't leave them behind.'

'But that means you'll stay there,' he cried. 'You'll never let them go through that again to come back to Britain.'

'Perhaps.' She tightened the lids on the bottles and sat on a stool, sighing. 'They'll hate being shut away.' She sent them a faintly guilty look this time, willing them to accept that she had no alternative.

He'd started pacing again and now he spun around. 'What about your work?' he said accusingly.

'I've explained to everyone as best as I can,' she said, her voice deliberately calm although the thought of leaving her clients had given her a lot of anguish. She managed a weak smile as she removed the muslin bag containing the remains of the sage and put it to one side for her compost. 'I don't understand why you're so upset about this, Alistair. You're hardly here these days and, besides, I promise you I'll get good tenants to be your new neighbours.'

'Make sure it's a short lease. At least if New Zealand doesn't work out you'll have somewhere to come back to,' he said heartily. 'Thank heavens you're not selling.'

'I could never sell,' she said tightly. 'Never.'

'Libby…?' He frowned, hesitated. 'You know…?'

Libby's alarm bells rang. Firmly she said, 'No, Alistair. Don't start that again. We're friends and I want to keep it that way. In your heart you know there's nothing deeper there.'

'That doesn't make it any easier to say goodbye. Even if I accept what you're saying, you're still my dearest friend.'

She laughed. 'What about that woman who came back with you from France last month? You two seemed fairly close.'

His cheeks flushed. 'I'm seeing her tomorrow,' he confessed. 'I'm taking her to the wedding.'

Libby sobered abruptly. The wedding. Nathan's wedding. She wasn't going to let herself think about that. She stood up again. 'I hope I've made enough of this,' she said worriedly, inspecting her two bottles. Monica's menopausal symptoms had been particularly bad recently and sage was the herb she responded to most rapidly. 'Do you think I should pick some more?'

'I don't know.' Alistair grinned, his good humour apparently restored by the thought of his blonde friend. 'Chuck in a bit more vodka,' he advised. 'That stuff will cure anything.'

'Perhaps I should try it myself,' she muttered under her breath, only half joking as she rinsed out her wine press.

But Alistair's hearing was clearly acute and his brow furrowed worriedly. 'You're not sick, are you, Libby? That's not the reason for this sudden mad dash to see the world?'

'I'm as fit as a fiddle,' she told him. Physically at least, she added to herself. 'And there's nothing sudden about this. I've been thinking about it for months.' For two months, she thought precisely. It had been two months exactly since that dreadful afternoon in Nathan's office.

'You've lost weight,' he said assessingly, his eyes suddenly sharp. 'And you're too pale.'

'I'm fine.' She dried the press then replaced it in her cupboard and flicked her hair back over her shoulders to get it out of her way. 'Stop fussing.'

He brightened. '"Stop fussing",' he repeated. 'That's exactly what Nathan said to me this morning.'

Libby froze, not wanting to hear this, but, oblivious to her feelings, he said, 'I'm best man but there's been no rehearsal, no meetings, nothing. I don't even know what I'm supposed to do so I called him this morning to say I'd come down early in the morning for a rehearsal, but he says there'll be no time. He's working until lunchtime at least and going straight from work to the register office. He'll meet me there.' He grinned. 'Only Nathan,' he said ruefully, 'would work on his own wedding day. I almost feel sorry for his bride.'

'You just have to do the ring thing, don't you?' Libby said stiffly, feeling her nails starting to dig into her palms. 'Then a speech afterwards.'

'I hope so.' He gave a mock shudder. 'Mother says this Paula woman seems very particular. Hope I don't get off to a bad start with her by mucking anything up.'

'You'll be fine.' But *she* wouldn't be if this conversation continued. 'I've some shopping to do,' she said briskly. 'Anything you want from town?'

'Nothing.' Alistair glanced at his watch and his mouth twisted. 'Sorry. I didn't mean to rabbit on.'

She kept her face very still and he made his way to the door. 'I just wish you'd told me earlier about your plans,' he continued. 'You've only left me two weeks to change your mind.'

Libby shook her head. To her despair, two months without Nathan had done nothing to dull her love or longing for him. Every car in the lane sent her racing to the window, every sound from Alistair's cottage sent excitement washing through her. The solution seemed to be to go somewhere where she'd be forced to accept that there was no chance of seeing him again.

'Nothing will change my mind, Alistair.' She followed him through to her kitchen. 'I might be late back,' she said, forcing herself to add politely, 'I hope you have a great time tomorrow.'

'You mean try not to make a mess of things,' he said easily. 'I'll be home on Monday with the full story.'

'I'll see you then.' It felt as if her insides were shrivelling. 'Bye.'

On his way to St Stephen's for his Saturday round the next morning Nathan stopped at Mr McTaggart's flat near King's Cross. One of the district nurses had been calling daily but Nathan still visited once a week, intrigued by the change in the lesions he'd feared would never improve. The healing wasn't miraculous, by any means, but in this case any difference was important.

In the last seven days the smallest ulcer had almost healed and the largest defect had certainly shrunk a little. Nathan grinned as he changed the bandages. 'You're doing all right,' he said easily.

'Aye.' Mr McTaggart beamed at him. 'And we managed a wee walk yesterday to the park.' He let the leg of his trousers fall to cover the bandages. 'You'll stay for a drink, then?'

Nathan checked his watch. 'Ten minutes,' he agreed. 'I'm due at the hospital.'

'You work too hard,' his patient's wife said as she brought in their drinks on a tray. 'All doctors work too hard.' She poured her husband and herself tea from a fine china teapot, then passed Nathan's coffee across. 'I suppose that's all you'll be doing today, working?'

He took a mouthful of hot liquid but was startled to hear himself saying, 'Not at all. I'm getting married this afternoon.'

Both his hosts gasped in astonishment, then Mr McTaggart chuckled. 'Greatest day of your life,' he wheezed. 'Well, it was for me.' The couple exchanged a look which, Nathan realised, could only be described as deeply loving. 'Sixty-two years we've been married, come September. Sixty-two years.'

His wife sighed. 'Such a special day,' she said, her face creasing dreamily so that for a moment she looked almost girlish. 'The beginning of your new life. You must be so excited.'

Was he? Nathan analysed his emotions and came up with 'resigned'. 'Sixty-two years and no regrets?' he asked carefully, not wanting to offend them but nevertheless curious.

Mr McTaggart's eyes twinkled as he patted his wife's frail hand. 'None that have lasted through to the next morning,' he said happily. 'Never go to sleep on an argument, that's what we've always said. Bed is for loving, not fighting.'

Nathan smiled, but inwardly he was aware of a growing discomfort within him. His bed had not exactly been a place for loving recently. Fortunately Paula seemed to have assumed he'd been struck down by an old-fashioned determination to wait until after the wedding and had made allowances accordingly.

'Loving, not fighting,' he repeated. 'I'll remember that.' Deliberately he checked his watch and stood up. 'Time to go.' He replaced his cup and saucer on the tray. 'Thanks for coffee.' He collected his bag. 'Look after those legs and I'll see you next week.'

'You're not taking a honeymoon, then?'

'I'm too busy at the moment.' He'd decided it wasn't fair to expect his colleagues to cover for him so soon after his last leave, and although Paula had seemed mildly irritated about missing the Mediterranean holiday she'd planned she hadn't actually objected. He signalled for his patient to stay where he was rather than escort him to the door. 'Perhaps in a few months.'

At the front door Mrs McTaggart took his arm, her squeeze surprisingly strong considering her size. 'You have a wonderful day,' she said gruffly, and to his astonishment he saw there were tears in her eyes. 'We'll be thinking of you.'

Nathan strode to his car, uncomfortably aware he felt like a fraud and angered by that feeling. He *was* getting married and he was going to make sure the marriage worked. He started the engine but instead of pulling away he leaned forward, gripping the steering-wheel. Sixty-two years? The figure played over and over in his mind. In sixty-two years, if he and Paula lived that long, would he honestly be able to say he had no regrets?

Briefly he let himself think of Libby. He pictured her rising from the sea. He remembered the sweet womanliness of her smile that morning she'd undressed for him in her kitchen.

Abruptly he slammed the Saab into gear. He'd chosen the only responsible path and it was too late for second thoughts. In a few short hours he'd be married to Paula.

CHAPTER THIRTEEN

As NATHAN reversed the Saab into a park outside the register office just before two, he caught a glimpse of his set face in the windscreen mirror. He scowled. 'Lighten up, Nathan,' he said roughly. 'This is what you wanted. This is what's supposed to put the world back to rights again.'

Seeing his family in all its noisy glory spilling down the steps of the town hall, it didn't improve his mood. Acknowledging the cheers and whistles with a wave, and neatly sidestepping two of Lucy's children who cavorted on the pavement, he made for his mother who stood off to one side with Kenneth.

'I said the two of you and Alistair, not the whole mob.' He frowned. 'Where *is* Alistair?'

She looked around. 'He's here somewhere,' she said vaguely. 'With his girlfriend.'

Nathan tensed. 'His girlfriend?'

'Mmm. You know.' She sent him a quick, assessing look, then said distantly, 'I'm sure you remember Libby.' Irritatingly she turned away to talk to Lucy, and in despair Nathan turned to her husband.

'Try inside,' Kenneth told him. 'Alistair muttered something about practising his speech.'

'Thanks.' Grimly Nathan made his way up the steps, his nerves so taut he could barely manage a smile for the twins' greetings as he made his way past them.

He found Alistair just inside the revolving doors of the town hall, a tall, blonde girl laughing beside him. Ignoring her, Nathan demanded, 'Where's Libby? Mother said Libby was here.'

But Alistair just blinked in dull, puzzled astonishment. 'Libby? You mean *my* Libby?'

'She's not *your* Libby,' he grated. 'She's not *your* anything.'

Hastily Alistair backed against the wall. 'W-wait a second, Nathan,' he stammered, holding his hands up as if to fend him off. 'I don't know what Mother's talking about, but if you mean Libby Deane then she's definitely not here.' He gave a quick, almost nervous smile at the girl, who was staring at Nathan as if she thought he'd gone mad. 'This is Cynthia, my date. Cynthia, this is Nathan, my brother. Nathan's the one who's getting married today.'

Nathan's fists clenched. 'Libby's not here,' he said dully.

'Of course not.' Alistair frowned, exchanging another worried look with the girl by his side. 'Nathan, are you OK?' When Nathan said nothing, Alistair chuckled nervously. 'I get it,' he said tensely. 'Pre-wedding nerves.'

'I'll see you outside,' the blonde girl said hastily, her singsong voice tinged with an accent Nathan couldn't spare the time to place. She kissed Alistair on the cheek before giving Nathan a briefly curious look and escaping through the doors, leaving them alone.

Immediately Nathan blurted, 'Is she all right?' At his brother's obvious bewilderment he added irritably, 'Libby!'

Alistair blinked again then said in a subdued voice, as if he suddenly understood everything, 'Oh. So I was right that night at the anniversary.' He grimaced. 'Libby denied it but I shouldn't have let her persuade me.' He leaned back against the wall, seeming to need its support. 'If you must know, no, she isn't all right,' he said quietly, his voice tinged with indignation. 'She's lost weight, she looks like a ghost and she's emigrating. To New Zealand.'

'New Zealand?' Nathan felt as if all the air had been sucked out of his lungs. 'But Cornwall…the cottage. She loves it there. It's her home. She belongs there.' He couldn't imagine her anywhere else.

'She's running away.' There was bitter resentment in the eyes Alistair lifted to him. 'I presume from you.'

Nathan looked away, acknowledging his guilt and there was a brief, taut silence before Alistair spoke again. 'I hope like hell you know what you're doing, Nate,' he said, looking outside to the long white car which was pulling up on the road outside, 'because your bride's just arrived.'

It had been a warm, sunny afternoon. Perfect, Libby thought faintly as she clambered down the cliff path that evening, for a wedding.

Stripping off her cotton shorts and T-shirt, she ran towards the waves and dived in, swimming furiously across to the far side of the bay, experiencing the cool water against her bare body as a sort of dull pleasure, as much enjoyment as she could expect on such a day.

It was late now, almost dark, and she wondered what they were doing. Were they still at the reception? Her stomach clenched. Or had they left early, anxious to…consummate their marriage?

She groaned aloud, knowing it was useless trying to force her thoughts to other things. Nathan was completely and utterly lost to her now and although she'd known that for weeks nothing had seemed so irreversibly final until today.

Getting on that plane to New Zealand, that would be the next step in her healing, she acknowledged, steeling herself for the pain of leaving. Until then she had to just try and get through each day at a time.

Determined that for this one night at least she wouldn't lie awake until dawn, imagining him with his new wife, she swam fiercely back and forth across the bay until her body was exhausted. Then, before swimming back to the beach, she paused, treading water to catch her breath, her gaze drawn to the cottage which in two weeks she'd be seeing for the last time.

On the top of the cliff she saw movement. Her gaze sharpened. A man, she realised, her breath locking in her throat. There was a man up there. His head shifted and she gasped aloud, for even though it was too dark to see him properly the sensation as his eyes locked with hers was unmistakable.

Nathan. Her concentration so utter she missed a wave and it caught her awkwardly, splashing over her face and submerging her, but when she surfaced he was still there.

Nathan. She tilted her head. She was hallucinating. Calmly she considered whether that meant she'd gone mad. She wondered whether she'd still hallucinate about him in New Zealand. Perhaps travelling all that way wouldn't be enough of an escape after all.

But then her hallucination moved again, turning towards the path, and she realised he looked very real. Too real. 'Oh, no,' she moaned, beginning to swim towards the beach. Surely he hadn't been cruel enough to bring his bride to Cornwall for their honeymoon?

He was waiting for her on the beach with her cats. As the water became shallower she waded up onto the sand. As she approached, William and Duncan left them, strolling towards the path, but Nathan stood very still, very dark, very formal in his morning suit, a bow-tie hanging loosely around his neck.

Silently he retrieved her towel and held it out to her, and she took it equally quietly and wound it around herself, taking care not to let their hands touch.

'Libby, I've been running away from the way I feel about you since the first moment I saw you,' he said deeply. 'I don't want to run any more.'

Libby tucked, then untucked, then retucked the corner of

her towel under her arm, her movements tense and agitated, not knowing what to say.

He shoved his hands into his pockets with a violence that suggested he was either frustrated or angry with himself. 'Libby, listen to me.' His voice was urgent but in the darkening light a quick glance revealed his expression to be brooding and unreadable.

'I hurt you, not deliberately but because I simply didn't recognise that the way I felt about you was more than a sexual obsession. I left you here, then in London I sent you away because I genuinely thought both times that that was the best thing for you, but now I regret that. I'm sorry.'

He was sorry. She turned away from him, her shoulders sagging with despair as she trudged wearily towards the path. He'd come to apologise, but didn't he understand he was only making things harder for her?

'Libby!' He followed her, demanding she stop, but she was determined to ignore him—would have ignored him if it hadn't been for the hands that took her shoulders and hauled her shuddering body back against him. 'Libby, you said you loved me,' he said hoarsely. 'Have I destroyed that?'

'Nathan, go away,' she said sadly, closing her eyes weakly at the heat that radiated from him and flooded through her body. 'Please, go away. I can't bear this.'

'I can't leave you again,' he groaned, and she felt his mouth shifting in her damp hair. 'I can't go away. I love you.'

She shook her head, slowly, from side to side, keeping her eyes tightly closed. 'It was sex,' she said hollowly. 'That was all you wanted. I don't blame you for that.' But even if he wanted her again she couldn't go through with it. She couldn't share his bed, knowing he'd leave her again the way he always did.

Behind her he muttered something harsh. His grip on her

arms momentarily tightened, but then he released her again, his hands restlessly stroking her arms the way he'd stroked her up on the cliffs the day he'd told her that Alistair loved her.

'I was wrong when I said I didn't love you,' he rasped. 'I didn't understand that at the time but I was wrong. I thought it was best that you just went away and lived your life.'

'Well, I went.' She pushed him away and turned slowly to face him, determined that *he* go now. 'And I'm living my life. I accept that whatever we had is over,' she said, feeling no triumph at the way his shadowed face contorted as if her words hurt him. 'I won't be your mistress, Nathan. It's not right and it would destroy me. Go back to your wife.'

'I don't have a wife,' he said bleakly, tilting her chin with one gentle finger and compelling her to meet his shadowed eyes. 'I'm not married.'

Libby swallowed, the movement seeming complicated and awkward. 'But what about Paula?'

He lifted one broad shoulder impatiently, as if that didn't matter. 'Gone,' he said carelessly, although the way his eyes slid away from hers suggested he still bore his guilt about that less casually than he was pretending.

'Libby, it was never sex with us. There was always more. I just kept my mind too closed to recognise that. Those weeks here with you were the happiest weeks of my life. I thought pleasure like that could never last. But now I think it can. I think it can last years. Sixty, seventy years, whatever. I don't want to live without it. I do love you. I love you insanely. Life without you in it isn't good or sensible or fulfilled—it's barren and incomplete, and I don't want to live that way any longer.'

Libby didn't believe him. She saw the strain in him, felt

his tension and, despite her wretchedness, worried for him. Hoarsely she said, 'Did Paula stand you up?'

'No!' He shook his head, as if irritated by having to think about the other woman. 'Calling off the wedding was a mutual decision.' But as if he saw her frown and understood that she wouldn't be distracted, he went on, 'We'd both had doubts this past month but I'd been working such long hours to make up for my time away that we never had the chance to talk properly. Today at the register office we did. We talked. It was obvious to both of us that neither of us was going into marriage for the right reasons.'

Libby felt as if she were reeling. They'd called off the wedding? Nathan wasn't married? And he'd said he loved her? She sank to the sand, clutching her head, watching the way her sandy footprints slowly faded into the water. 'The right reasons?' she echoed.

At her quiet words Nathan eased himself down beside her, leaving a few inches of sand between them.

'Your beautiful suit,' she protested huskily, focusing on his shirt, his lapel—looking anywhere but at his shadowed face. 'The sand will ruin it.'

'Forget it.' He sounded impatient. 'Libby, Paula's never been in love with me. Just as I was never in love with her. I know to you that that must sound cold, but try and understand that our relationship was…convenient for both of us. And we work well together. I imagine neither of us would even have thought about marrying in the first place if it hadn't been for her thinking once that she might be pregnant. Once the idea was planted, it seemed to make sense. It seemed easier to let it happen than to fight it.

'After you left me that night I…I wanted my life to be normal again. I thought marrying Paula would make it that way. I was desperate for a solution. And I was her idea of a suitable accessory, but lately I haven't been behaving the way a good accessory should. I'd disappointed her. She was having second thoughts. She wanted me to go into private practice with her when we were married. I decided not to and she didn't like that. And she'd agreed to have children because I wanted them, but inside she really didn't want that.

'Today, finally, we both came to our senses. She left me as much as I left her. All I can do is be grateful it happened in time. The alternative would have had us both in a divorce court within months.'

When Libby stayed silent, he stroked the side of her bare arm. 'Because I couldn't have kept denying how much I wanted you,' he said urgently. 'Not for very much longer. I know this must seem insane when I was about to marry another woman, but I thought that that marriage, at least, would force me to keep my hands off you.'

She shook her head slowly, tracing idle patterns in the sand with unsteady fingers. 'But that isn't what I wanted,' she protested. 'Why did you?'

He removed his hand, dangling both of them restlessly over his knees. 'Libby, on my first night in Cornwall I watched you swimming. I wanted to run down to the beach and take you in my arms and make love to you until the end of the world. Seeing you after that, it only made that wanting worse. I'm not used to that. I'm not used to being at the mercy of my physical responses. I didn't like it. No, more than that—I hated it. It was as if I was being consumed by desire. It was too overwhelming for me to be aware of anything more. I was falling in love with you but the physical attraction was so strong that I didn't recognise anything apart from that.'

She said nothing and Nathan clenched his fists, unclenched them, clenched them again. 'My world was ordered before you, Libby. Disciplined and tidy. There were no surprises and no shocks and I thought I liked it like that.

Up until today it seemed desperately important that I kept it that way, but I was wrong.'

Her mouth felt impossibly dry and her voice came out as a croak. 'What's changed?'

She felt his gaze prickling the top of her lowered head.

'Today I realised that I barely understood why that control was so important to me,' he said slowly. 'You're all that matters to me now.'

Libby lifted her eyes, listening to the pounding of the inky water and the tinkling movements of the pebbles as the waves sucked them from the beach. 'You love me.'

'I adore you.' He moved suddenly, rolling her beneath him so he lay above her, his weight braced on his elbows. 'It feels as if I've loved you from that first night.'

Libby, flushing, was glad of the near darkness because it would conceal her colour. 'I didn't know you saw me swimming then,' she said huskily. 'I thought the cottage was deserted that night. Was I…wearing anything?'

'Nothing,' he interrupted huskily. 'Gloriously nothing. You were like a mermaid, emerging from the waves. After that I was lost. You had me completely and utterly bewitched.' His mouth nuzzled her heated neck, and she arched back, exposing more of it to him. 'You were enchanting. I wanted you madly.'

She eased him away, rolling onto her side to face him, needing to understand. 'I felt the same the first time I saw you, but I wasn't scared of that. Why were you?'

'Because I felt as if I was losing control. Because I thought you were too young and I thought Alistair was in love with you.' His hand came out and he stroked her cheek. 'I still think he's in love with you,' he added softly, 'and I still think you're far too young for me. But I don't care any more.'

For a few seconds they were both quiet and then he continued. 'You belong here, Libby, and I belong in London.

London's where my work is and I don't want to give that up. I've always known it wouldn't be fair to take you away from here.'

He kissed her throat. 'Alistair told me you're emigrating to New Zealand. That was because of…everything, wasn't it? We could go for a holiday if you want but you don't really want to leave here, do you?'

Libby shook her head, but the movement drew her hair across her face and her lashes fluttered as he tenderly lifted it away. 'I couldn't forget you,' she confessed. 'I thought going away as far as I possibly could would help.'

He grunted. 'I'd have followed you.'

'I belong with you,' she whispered, hearing his certainty and believing him.

'I'll be here every weekend I'm not on call,' he said hoarsely. 'Holidays. Some nights even during the week. If I fly all the time rather than drive I'll be able to make more time. I'll keep a car here to use. And if you ever want to, you can come up to London. We'll manage somehow.'

She didn't understand. 'You don't want me to live with you?'

'Of course I do.' He seemed astounded by the question. 'I want to marry you, love you, live with you always. But I can't ask you to leave here. This is you. This…beach, here, the cottage, this is where you belong, Libby. I know that.'

'I told you, I belong with you,' she insisted, understanding at last. 'Nathan, you accused me once of being a romantic, but it's you who's the romantic. I'm not some ethereal, fairy creature who can't survive away from this little place. I love my life here, yes, but I'd love anywhere if it meant I was with you. I was prepared to go twelve thousand miles away to forget you, Nathan. Don't you think that means I can manage London if it means being with you?'

'You…sweet, wonderful angel.' His mouth captured hers

in a long, lingering kiss. 'We'll come down at weekends,' he told her hoarsely. 'And every holiday, and we'll move somewhere bigger in London so you and the cats will have more space. You'll be able to work still. People will flock to you.'

'It's all right.' She swivelled onto her knees and brushed at the sandy lapel of his jacket. 'As I'll be staying, there's a course I'd like to attend,' she said softly. 'In London, where I attended the workshop. A degree course.' She flushed. 'They seem to think I'm suitable.'

'Of course you are.' He kissed her again, a hard, encouraging kiss that aroused her immediately. 'My beautiful academic,' he said gently, drawing away before she could kiss him back. 'You'll be top of the class. What about Duncan and Wills?'

'They'll be so relieved they don't have to go into quarantine that they'll go happily anywhere,' she reassured him. 'Also, they like you. They'll be fine.' She frowned slightly. 'Nathan, what about *your* work? Will me being with you in London interrupt that?'

He lay carelessly back in the sand. 'I don't know what Alistair has said to you,' he said quietly, 'but I don't consider myself a workaholic. My work and my patients are important to me, and it's easy to work every hour in the day if that's what you want to do, filling the hours with research and teaching. But with you at home I wouldn't need to do that. I realised today what will make me happy, and it's not being in control or working all hours of the day. It's you.'

'I love you.' She swooped down atop him, straddling his thighs with her knees. 'Kiss me and convince me properly.'

'Whatever, whenever, wherever you desire, my love.' His hands loosened the fastening of her towel and he lifted her forward onto him, his mouth warm and seeking her breasts.

They made love then, on the beach, beneath the stars, passionately, intensely. Afterwards they swam in the darkness before Nathan carried her up to the cottage and they made love again.

Later, much later, they talked again. He told her about his problems at work, about how he'd thought about leaving the NHS. 'In the last few months I've done things that have surprised me.' He shifted slightly, rolling on his side and gathering her to him. 'For which I blame you, my darling,' he murmured. 'After leaving you here, I barely cared one way or another whether I kept my job, and I was more outspoken than normal.'

He stroked her hair, burying his face in it, surrounding himself with it. 'But that recklessness helped,' he said against her ear. 'I achieved some concessions. My enjoyment and satisfaction comes from what I can do for my patients. While I can still do something useful for them I'll stay.'

Libby smiled. 'I'm glad you feel like that,' she said softly, speaking as someone who knew what it was like to feel useless within the system. They exchanged a long, loving kiss, and when he lifted his head she asked him about the wedding.

He collapsed back, closing his eyes. 'It was an absolute farce!' he groaned. 'The family was thrilled. They've been warning me for years that pressure of work would be the ruin of me eventually and seeing me crack up and run out on my own wedding—it was like Christmas and Easter rolled into one for them.' His mouth twitched. 'Mother was beside herself with joy but, of course, she knew it wasn't work. She played a trick on me and it worked. She knew I was coming to you,' he said, opening one eye to see her blush.

He rolled over, catching her beneath him. 'Today the world came right,' he said softly. 'Even if it wasn't in the way I was expecting. Today I realised that if I had sixty-two years to live I wasn't going to spend them just existing. I wanted to *live*. And living meant being with the woman I loved.'

Libby lifted her head, frowning. 'Sixty-two years?'

Nathan laughed. 'Another time,' he said lightly. 'I'll explain another time.' He lowered his mouth to hers again, teasing the corners of her lips until she opened to him. 'We've years of pleasure ahead of us,' he murmured softly, and he kissed her. 'Starting now.'

MILLS & BOON®
MEDICAL ROMANCE™

A FAMILY TO CARE FOR by Judy Campbell

Dr Sally Jones isn't quite sure what she wants next, so the locum post at the general practice in the Scottish Highlands will give her time to decide. Finding widowed Dr Rob Mackay there is not altogether a pleasant surprise, because he'd walked out on her in the past. This Rob is more serious, and the father of toddler twin boys, yet he attracts her as strongly as ever...

POTENTIAL HUSBAND by Lucy Clark
A follow on to Potential Daddy

When rural GP Vicky Hansen first met orthopaedic surgeon Steven Pearce, she was deeply attracted, but resigned to him returning to the city—until she found he'd bought some of her family land to renovate the cottage there. Meanwhile, he says, he will be her lodger!

FOR JODIE'S SAKE by Maggie Kingsley

Widowed for two years, Kate Rendall wants to start afresh, and takes the job offered by widower Dr Ethan Flett to care for his fourteen year old daughter, Jodie. Kate is shocked by the instant attraction she feels for Ethan, which is mutual, but while Jodie might like Kate as a carer, would she accept her as a mother?

Available from 7th April 2000

0003/03

MILLS & BOON®

MEDICAL ROMANCE™

DEFINITELY DADDY by Alison Roberts

Going back to work was exciting and hard for Harriet McKinlay. It meant putting her adored almost three year old, Freddie, in nursery. But why did the spinal unit boss, Patrick Miller, dislike her? She didn't know that Paddy had saved her life when she gave birth, or that he had the wrong idea about her morals!

TENDER LOVING CARE by Jennifer Taylor
Dalverston General Hospital

Midwife Sarah Harris had devoted herself to work, but the arrival of Dr Niall Gillespie, as new head of the department, changed all that. Except that Niall held everyone at bay—could she break down the barriers he had so carefully erected?

ONCE A WISH by Carol Wood
The first of two books

Dr Alissa Leigh, widowed with a small daughter, has been working at the health centre for a while when Dr Max Darvill and his son arrive. But Max's ex-wife is still very visible, and despite the friendship of the two children, Alissa isn't convinced that Max is really free to love her…

Available from 7th April 2000

Available at most branches of WH Smith, Tesco, Martins, Borders, Easons, Volume One/James Thin and most good paperback bookshops

0003/03b

FREE

4 BOOKS
AND A SURPRISE GIFT!

We would like to take this opportunity to thank you for reading this Mills & Boon® book by offering you the chance to take FOUR more specially selected titles from the Medical Romance™ series absolutely FREE! We're also making this offer to introduce you to the benefits of the Reader Service™—

- ★ FREE home delivery
- ★ FREE monthly Newsletter
- ★ FREE gifts and competitions
- ★ Exclusive Reader Service discounts
- ★ Books available before they're in the shops

Accepting these FREE books and gift places you under no obligation to buy; you may cancel at any time, even after receiving your free shipment. Simply complete your details below and return the entire page to the address below. *You don't even need a stamp!*

YES! Please send me 4 free Medical Romance books and a surprise gift. I understand that unless you hear from me, I will receive 6 superb new titles every month for just £2.40 each, postage and packing free. I am under no obligation to purchase any books and may cancel my subscription at any time. The free books and gift will be mine to keep in any case.

MOEC

Ms/Mrs/Miss/Mr ....Initials ....
BLOCK CAPITALS PLEASE

Surname ....

Address ....

....

....Postcode ....

Send this whole page to:
UK: FREEPOST CN81, Croydon, CR9 3WZ
EIRE: PO Box 4546, Kilcock, County Kildare (stamp required)

Offer valid in UK and Eire only and not available to current Reader Service subscribers to this series. We reserve the right to refuse an application and applicants must be aged 18 years or over. Only one application per household. Terms and prices subject to change without notice. Offer expires 30th September 2000. As a result of this application, you may receive further offers from Harlequin Mills & Boon Limited and other carefully selected companies. If you would prefer not to share in this opportunity please write to The Data Manager at the address above.

Mills & Boon® is a registered trademark owned by Harlequin Mills & Boon Limited.
Medical Romance™ is being used as a trademark.